GEORGES SIMENON

Maigret and the Nahour Case

Translated by WILLIAM HOBSON

PENGUIN BOOKS

PENGUIN CLASSICS

UK | USA | Canada | Ireland | Australia
India | New Zealand | South Africa

Penguin Books is part of the Penguin Random House group of companies
whose addresses can be found at global.penguinrandomhouse.com.

Penguin
Random House
UK

First published in French as *Maigret et l'affaire Nahour*
by Presses de la Cité 1966
This translation first published 2019
002

Set in 12.5/15 pt Dante MT Std
Typeset by Jouve (UK), Milton Keynes
Printed and bound in Great Britain by Clays Ltd, Elcograf S.p.A.

ISBN: 978-0-241-30415-0

www.greenpenguin.co.uk

PENGUIN CLASSICS

Maigret and the Nahour Case

'Extraordinary masterpieces of the twentieth century'
– John Banville

'A brilliant writer' – India Knight

'Intense atmosphere and resonant detail . . . make Simenon's fiction remarkably like life' – Julian Barnes

'A truly wonderful writer . . . marvellously readable – lucid, simple, absolutely in tune with the world he creates'
– Muriel Spark

'Few writers have ever conveyed with such a sure touch, the bleakness of human life' – A. N. Wilson

'Compelling, remorseless, brilliant' – John Gray

'A writer of genius, one whose simplicity of language creates indelible images that the florid stylists of our own day can only dream of' – *Daily Mail*

'The mysteries of the human personality are revealed in all their disconcerting complexity' – Anita Brookner

'One of the greatest writers of our time' – *The Sunday Times*

'I love reading Simenon. He makes me think of Chekhov'
– William Faulkner

'One of the great psychological novelists of this century'
– *Independent*

'The greatest of all, the most genuine novelist we have had in literature' – André Gide

'Simenon ought to be spoken of in the same breath as Camus, Beckett and Kafka' – *Independent on Sunday*

Maigret and the Nahour Case

1.

He was struggling, forced to defend himself because someone had unexpectedly grabbed hold of his shoulder. He even tried to throw a punch and had the humiliating feeling that his arm wasn't responding but just lay limp at his side as though paralysed.

'Who's that?' he shouted, vaguely aware that it wasn't the right question exactly.

Had he even really made a sound?

'Jules! The telephone . . .'

He had definitely heard something, a noise that sounded threatening in his sleep, but it hadn't occurred to him for a moment that it was the telephone ringing and that he was in bed, in the middle of an unpleasant dream that he had already forgotten, and being shaken awake by his wife.

He automatically reached out a hand for the receiver, opening his eyes and sitting up as he did so. Madame Maigret was sitting in the warm bed with him, and the lamp on her side was giving out a soft, cosy light.

'Hello,' he said.

'Who is that?' he almost blurted out, as if he were still dreaming.

'Maigret? It's Pardon here.'

Maigret managed to make out the time on the alarm-clock on his wife's bedside table. It was 1.30 a.m. They had left the Pardons just after eleven, after their monthly dinner, which on this occasion had consisted of a delicious stuffed shoulder of mutton.

'Yes. Go ahead.'

'Sorry to wake you, you must have been fast asleep. Something's just happened here, something pretty serious, I think, that comes under your jurisdiction.'

The Maigrets and Pardons had been friends for over ten years, taking it in turns to invite one another for dinner once a month, and yet it had never crossed either man's mind to call the other by his Christian name.

'I'm listening, Pardon. Go on.'

The voice on the other end of the line was anxious, embarrassed.

'I think it would be better if you came and saw me. You'd understand the situation better.'

'There hasn't been an accident, I hope?'

A hesitation.

'No. Not exactly, but I'm worried.'

'Is your wife all right?'

'Yes. She's just making us some coffee.'

Madame Maigret was looking inquiringly at her husband, trying to figure out what was going on from his replies.

'I'll come right away . . .'

He hung up. He was fully awake now, with a look of concern on his face. This was the first time Doctor Pardon had called him like that, and Maigret knew him well enough to understand it must be serious.

'What's happening?'

'I don't know. Pardon needs me.'

'Why didn't he come and see you?'

'I need to go there for some reason.'

'He was very cheerful earlier. So was his wife. We talked about his daughter and son-in-law, the cruise they're planning to take next summer around the Balearics . . .'

Was Maigret listening? He felt uneasy as he got dressed, wondering in spite of himself what might have caused the doctor's telephone call.

'I'll go and make some coffee.'

'No need. Madame Pardon is making us some.'

'Shall I call a taxi?'

'There won't be one free in this weather, or, if you do, it will take half an hour to get here.'

It was 14 January – Friday 14 January – and it had been minus 12 in Paris all day. Snow had been falling heavily for the past few days, freezing so hard that it was impossible to clear, and despite the salt spread on the pavements, there were still patches of black ice that sent pedestrians sprawling.

'Put on your big scarf.'

A thick woollen scarf she had knitted for him which he almost never needed to wear.

'Don't forget your gumboots. I don't suppose you'll let me come with you, will you?'

'Why?'

She didn't like seeing him set off on his own tonight. On their way back from the Pardons, despite their both taking care, watching where they put their feet, Maigret had fallen heavily on the corner of Rue du Chemin-Vert and remained sitting on the ground for a while, feeling dazed and ashamed of himself.

'Did you hurt yourself?'

'No. I just got a bit of a shock, that's all.'

He had refused to let her help him up or take his arm when he finally got to his feet.

'No need for us both to fall over.'

She followed him to the door, kissed him and murmured:

'Be careful . . .'

She left the door half-open until he got to the ground floor. Maigret avoided Rue du Chemin-Vert, where he had fallen over earlier, taking the slightly longer route along Boulevard Richard-Lenoir to Boulevard Voltaire, where the Pardons lived.

He walked slowly, hearing no one else's footsteps. There were no taxis or cars in sight. Paris seemed deserted, and he could only remember seeing it like this, so frozen and snowbound, once or perhaps twice before in his life.

On Boulevard Voltaire, though, a truck was parked at the République end, its engine idling, and a few black figures were bustling about: workmen scattering spades-ful of salt over the road.

Lights could be seen in two of the Pardons' windows, the only windows illuminated in the entire block. Maigret made out a figure behind the curtains and when he reached the door, it opened before he could ring the bell.

'Sorry again, Maigret.'

Doctor Pardon was wearing the same navy-blue jacket as at dinner.

'I've got myself into such a tricky situation, I don't know what to do.'

As they went up in the lift, Maigret saw his features were drawn.

'Haven't you been to bed?'

In an embarrassed voice, the doctor explained:

'I didn't feel tired when you left so I decided to catch up on some of the paperwork I'm behind on.'

In other words, despite having to work, he hadn't wanted to put off their traditional dinner.

As it happened, the Maigrets had stayed later than usual. They had talked mainly about holidays, with Pardon observing that his patients were more and more exhausted when they came back from them these days, especially when they had been on package tours.

They passed through the waiting room, in which only a small light was on, and, instead of going on to the living room, turned into Pardon's surgery.

Madame Pardon appeared immediately with a tray and two cups, a coffee-pot and some sugar.

'Please forgive my appearance, I haven't even taken the time to get dressed. I'm not staying, though. My husband's the one who needs to talk to you.'

She was wearing a pale-blue dressing gown over her nightdress, her feet in slippers.

'He didn't want to bother you. I insisted and, if that was wrong of me, I'm sorry.'

She poured out the coffee and headed for the door.

'I shan't go to sleep before you're finished, so don't hesitate to call me if you need anything. You're not hungry, are you, Maigret?'

'I had too good a dinner to be hungry.'

'You aren't, either?'

'No, thank you.'

An open door gave on to the little room in which the doctor examined his patients. In the middle there was a high folding table covered with a bloodstained sheet, and Maigret noticed some large bloodstains on the green linoleum.

'Sit down. Have your coffee first.'

He pointed to a stack of papers and index cards on his desk.

'You see. People don't realize that on top of consultations and visits we have all sorts of bureaucracy to take care of. Urgent calls are always coming in, so we put it off until we end up completely swamped. I was planning to spend two or three hours on this task.'

Pardon began his house calls at eight in the morning, then his surgery opened at ten. Picpus was not a rich part of town. It was a lower-middle-class neighbourhood, and you'd often see as many as fifteen people at a time in his waiting room. Maigret could count on the fingers of one hand the monthly dinners that hadn't been interrupted by a telephone call summoning Pardon away for an hour or more.

'I was engrossed in this paperwork. My wife was asleep. I didn't hear a thing until suddenly the doorbell rang, startling me. When I opened the door, I found a couple on the landing who seemed odd somehow.'

'Why?'

'Mainly because I didn't know either of them, the man or the woman. Generally if I'm disturbed in the middle of the night, it'll be one of my regular patients, one of those who don't have a telephone.'

'I see.'

'I also had the sense they didn't live locally. The woman was wearing a sealskin coat and matching hat. My wife had happened to be looking through a fashion magazine a couple of days ago and she'd suddenly said:

' "Next time you get me a coat, choose sealskin, not mink. Mink has become so common these days, but sealskin . . ."

'I didn't listen to the rest, but that came back to me as I was holding the door open, looking at them in surprise.

'The man's get-up was also not the sort of thing you usually see on Boulevard Voltaire.

'He did the talking, asking with a slight accent:

' "Doctor Pardon?"

' "That's me, yes."

' "This lady has just been hurt, and I'd like you to examine her."

' "How did you get my address?"

' "An old woman walking down Boulevard Voltaire gave it to us. She must have been a patient of yours."

'They had come into my surgery. The woman was very pale, as if she was about to faint, and she was staring at me with big, expressionless eyes, both hands clasped to her chest.

' "I think you should hurry, doctor," said the man, taking off his gloves.

' "What sort of injury is it?"

'Turning to the woman, who was very blonde and must have been just under thirty, he said:

' "You'd better take off your coat."

'Without a word, she took off her fur coat, and I saw that the back of her straw-coloured dress was soaked in blood down to the waist.

'Look, there's a bloodstain on the carpet next to my desk where she stood shaking.

'I showed her into the consulting room and asked her to take off her dress. I offered to help but, still without saying a word, she shook her head and got undressed herself.

'The man hadn't come in with us, but the door between the two rooms was still open, and he went on talking to me, or rather answering my questions. I had put on my coat, then washed my hands. The woman was lying motionless on her stomach, not making a sound.'

'What time was this?' asked Maigret, who had just lit his first pipe since the telephone call.

'I looked at the clock when the doorbell rang. It said ten past one. All this was very quick; telling you about it takes far longer.

'In fact, I was already washing the wound and staunching the blood before I really realized what was happening. At first sight the wound didn't seem too bad. It was in her back, on the right-hand side: a gash about eight centimetres long that was still bleeding.

'As I got on with it, I carried on talking to the man, who was in my office, where I couldn't see him:

' "Tell me what happened."

' "I was walking down Boulevard Voltaire, a hundred metres from here, and this woman was walking in front of me."

' "You're not going to tell me she slipped?"

' "No. I was pretty surprised to see her alone in the street at that time of night and I slowed down so as not to give her the impression that I wanted to accost her. That's when I heard a car engine . . ." '

Pardon broke off to drink his coffee and pour himself a second cup.

'Do you want some?'

'Yes, please.'

Maigret was still sleepy, his eyelids were stinging, and he felt he was coming down with a head cold. Ten of his inspectors were in bed with flu, which had made his job considerably more complicated in the past few days.

'I am repeating our conversation as exactly as possible but I can't guarantee every word. I found that the wound was deeper between the third and fourth rib and as I was disinfecting it, something fell on the floor, although I didn't immediately take any notice.'

'A bullet?'

'Hang on. The man in the next room went on:

' "When the car drew level with this lady, it slowed down, not that it was driving that fast to start with. I saw an arm reach out of the door . . ." '

'The front door or back door?' Maigret interrupted.

'He didn't say, and I didn't think to ask. Don't forget I was performing an actual surgical procedure. It happens occasionally, when there's an emergency, but it's not my speciality, and I found the whole business strange. What surprised me most was the patient's complete silence.

'The man went on:

' "I heard a gunshot and I saw this person stagger, try to hold on to the front of a building, then give way at the knees and slowly crumple into the snow.

' "The car had already driven off and turned right into some street, I don't know what it's called.

' "I rushed forward. I saw she wasn't dead, and she managed to cling on to me and get back to her feet unaided.

' "I asked her if she was hurt and she nodded."

' "Didn't she talk to you?"

' "No. I didn't know what to do. I looked around for help. An old woman was passing, and I asked her if she knew where I could find a doctor. She pointed out your building and told me your name." '

Pardon fell silent, looking at Maigret like a guilty child.

Maigret asked the obvious question:

'Hadn't it occurred to him to take her to a hospital?'

'I pointed that out, saying that Saint-Antoine's is around the corner. He just muttered:

' "I didn't know." '

'Didn't he know the station is a hundred metres away either?'

'I suppose not. I felt in an awkward position. I knew I wasn't allowed to treat a gunshot wound without immediately informing the police, but then again, I'd started the procedure. I explained:

' "I'm just giving her first aid and when I've finished I'll call an ambulance."

'I applied a temporary dressing.

' "I can lend you a bathrobe so you don't have to put your bloodstained clothes back on."

'She shook her head and a few minutes later she got dressed again and rejoined the man she had come with in my office.

'I said to both of them:

' "Take a seat. I'll be with you in a minute."

'I wanted to take off my rubber gloves and my stained coat and reseal the bottles I had been using. I went on talking.

' "You'll have to give me your names and addresses. If you prefer a private clinic to a hospital, tell me so I can make arrangements . . ." '

Maigret had already guessed what had happened.

'How long were they out of your sight?'

'It's difficult to say exactly. I remember I picked up the bullet that had fallen on the ground while I was operating and threw the bloody swabs and towel in the basket . . . Two or three minutes? I went over to the door as I was talking and saw my office was empty.

'First I rushed out to the waiting room, then on to the landing. I couldn't hear the lift or anyone on the stairs, so I came back in here and looked out of the window but I couldn't see the pavement at the foot of the building.

'That's when I distinctly heard a car drive off. From the sound of it I'd swear it was powerful, a big sports car. By the time I'd opened the window, Boulevard Voltaire was empty except for a salt truck at the République end and a solitary passer-by some way off in the other direction.'

★

Apart from his closest colleagues such as Lucas, Janvier, Torrence and, more recently, young Lapointe, of whom Maigret was genuinely fond, Dr Pardon was his only friend.

The two men were the same age, give or take a year, and spent their days dealing with the maladies of individuals and society, so they had plenty in common.

They could talk for untold hours after their monthly dinners at Boulevard Richard-Lenoir and Boulevard Voltaire and the experiences they described were very similar.

Was it the respect they felt for each other that prevented them from using their first names? Tonight, in the peace and quiet of the doctor's office, they weren't as relaxed as they had been a few hours earlier, perhaps because chance was bringing them together in a professional capacity for the first time.

The doctor was in a funk and spoke faster than usual. He seemed anxious to prove his good faith, as he would if he were being questioned by the Medical Council.

Maigret meanwhile refrained from asking too many questions, restricting himself to those he considered absolutely necessary, and only after a slight hesitation.

'Tell me, Pardon, you said at the start that the man and woman didn't seem to be locals.'

The doctor tried to explain.

'My patients are mainly shopkeepers, artisans and ordinary folk. I am not a fashionable doctor or a specialist, I'm the sort that lugs his bag up five or six flights of stairs because there's no lift twenty times a day. There are smart, monied apartment blocks on my boulevard, but I've never seen anyone in the street like this evening's patients.

'The woman may not have said a word, but I still feel she was a foreigner. She looked very Nordic, with that milky complexion and fair hair you hardly ever see in Paris unless it's dyed, which hers wasn't. I think it highly probable, judging by her breasts, that she has had one or more children whom she breastfed.'

'Any distinguishing marks?'

'No . . . Wait . . . A scar about two centimetres long running from her left eye towards her ear. I noticed it because it looked like a sort of crow's foot, which is rather fetching in a very young face.'

'Do you think she kept silent voluntarily?'

'I'd swear she did. Just as, when I saw them on the landing and then in my office, I would have sworn that they knew each other, even intimately. This may be foolish, but I think there's a sort of aura around couples who are genuinely in love and that even when they're not looking at each other, when they're not touching each other, you can feel a bond between them.'

'Tell me about him.'

'I saw him more briefly, and he had an overcoat that he didn't take off, made of some soft, smooth fabric.'

'Was he wearing a hat?'

'No. He was bare-headed. Brown hair, fine features, tanned skin, brown eyes, darker than the regular hazel. I'd put his age at twenty-five or twenty-six and, from the way he talked, his manner and his clothes, I'd be inclined to say that he had always moved in privileged circles. A handsome boy, gentle-looking, slightly melancholic. Probably Spanish or South American.

'What should I do now? I don't know their names so I can't fill in their medical cards . . . I'd say it probably was a case of criminal assault.'

'Did you believe the man's story?'

'I didn't give it a second thought at the time. It was only when I found the office empty, and as I was waiting for you after I called, that I thought his explanation seemed strange.'

Maigret studied the bullet carefully.

'Probably from a 6.35. A gun that's only really dangerous at close range and generally not very accurate.'

'That explains the wound. The bullet had struck her back at an angle, grazing the skin for a few centimetres before penetrating enough to lodge between two ribs.'

'Can the woman go far in her condition?'

'I can't tell. I wonder if she took a sedative before coming here because she hardly reacted, even though superficial wounds are often the most painful.'

'Listen, Pardon,' Maigret grunted as he stood up, 'I'll try to deal with them. Send me a report tomorrow morning, repeating what you've just told me.'

'I won't be in trouble, will I?'

'It's your duty to help people at risk, isn't it?'

He lit a fresh pipe before putting on his gloves and his hat.

'I'll let you know.'

He went back out into the icy air and, looking intently at the snow piled up against the buildings, walked a hundred or so metres without seeing any bloodstains or signs of a fall. Retracing his steps, he then crossed Place Léon-Blum and went into the police station on the ground floor of the town hall.

He had known Sergeant Demarie, who was sitting behind the counter, for years.

'Hello, Demarie.'

Surprised to see the head of the Crime Squad suddenly appearing out of nowhere, the sergeant stood up with an embarrassed look because he had been reading a comic.

'Hello, Louvelle.'

Sergeant Louvelle was making coffee on a spirit stove.

'Did either of you hear anything about an hour ago?'

'No, detective chief inspector.'

'Something like a gunshot, a hundred metres from here?'

'No, nothing.'

'Between one and ten past one.'

'Which direction?'

'Boulevard Voltaire, the République end.'

'A two-man patrol, Officers Mathis and Bernier, went out at one on the dot, and took Boulevard Voltaire en route to Rue Amelot.'

'Where are they now?'

Demarie glanced at the electric clock.

'Around Bastille, unless they have already turned into Rue de la Roquette. The two men will be back at three. Do you want us to try and get hold of them?'

'No. Call me a taxi. Ring me at the Police Judiciaire when they're here.'

It took two or three telephone calls to find a free taxi. Maigret then called Boulevard Richard-Lenoir.

'Don't worry if I'm not back until the early hours . . . I'm at the local station . . . A taxi's coming to get me . . . Of course not! He's got nothing to do with what's happened . . . I've got to see to it tonight, though . . . No, I haven't fallen over. See you soon.'

The taxi passed the salt truck, which was inching its way forward, and they came across at most three cars before reaching Quai des Orfèvres, where the guard at the gate looked frozen stiff.

Upstairs he found Lucas with Inspectors Jussieu and Lourtie. Otherwise the offices appeared empty.

'Evening, boys. Stop whatever you're doing and ring round all the hospitals and private clinics in Paris. I want to know whether two people, a man and a woman, came in after one o'clock tonight. The woman, who's been shot in the back, may have come in on her own. Here's their description.'

He tried to repeat Pardon's exact words.

'Start with the east of town.'

As the three men rushed to the telephones, he went into his office, turned on the light and took off his overcoat and thick knitted scarf.

He didn't believe the story of a shot being fired from a passing car. That was a tactic gangsters used, and he'd never seen a gangster with a 6.35. Besides, only one shot had been fired, and that was pretty unusual for a shooting from a car. Like Pardon, he was certain the man and woman knew one another. Didn't the fact that they had sneaked out without a word, like accomplices, while the doctor was in his tiny consulting room for a few seconds, prove it?

He went back out to the three men, who had nearly got to the end of their list.

'Still nothing?'

'Nothing, chief.'

He called the emergency services himself.

'You didn't get any calls around one in the morning, did you? Someone reporting a gunshot.'

'Wait a minute, I'll ask my colleagues.'

A few moments later:

'Just a brawl and a stabbing in a bar at Porte d'Italie. Ambulance call-outs for broken legs and arms. It's easing up now that most people have gone home, but we're still getting a call roughly every ten minutes.'

He had barely hung up before Lucas called him over.

'Telephone for you, chief.'

It was Demarie from the eleventh arrondissement.

'The patrol's just got back. Mathis and Bernier didn't see anything out of the ordinary and only reported a few falls on the ice. Mathis did notice a red Alfa Romeo parked outside 76a, Boulevard Voltaire, however. He even said to his colleague: "We should have one of those to do our beat in."'

'What time was it?'

'Between five and ten past one. Mathis touched the bonnet out of habit and noticed it was still warm.'

In other words, the man and woman had just gone into the building, where they had rung the doctor's doorbell at ten past one.

How did they know Pardon's address? Mathis had been asked about the old woman and said he hadn't seen anyone of that description anywhere on the street.

Where had the couple come from? Why had they stopped on Boulevard Voltaire specifically, almost directly opposite a police station?

It was too late to alert the radio cars because the red car would have had time to reach its destination, wherever that might be.

Maigret was muttering away, frowning and taking little pulls on his pipe, while Lucas tried to guess what he was saying to himself.

'Foreigners . . . He was Latin-looking . . . The woman didn't say anything . . . because she can't speak French? Nordic-looking . . . but why Boulevard Voltaire and why Pardon?'

That's what bothered him most. If the couple lived in Paris they were bound to have an apartment in one of the smart neighbourhoods, and there were doctors on almost every street in the city. If the shot had been fired in an apartment building, why didn't they call a doctor rather than drag the wounded woman around town in sub-zero temperatures?

What if they were staying in a big hotel? . . . It was unlikely. The noise of a gunshot rarely went unnoticed in such places.

'Why are you looking at me like that?' he snapped at Lucas, apparently only just realizing he was standing opposite him.

'I'm waiting for you to tell me what to do.'

'What makes you think I know?'

Maigret smiled, amused by his own truculence.

'It's all pretty far-fetched, and I don't know where to start. Not to mention that I was woken up by the telephone in the middle of some nightmare or other.'

'Do you want some coffee?'

'I'll go out and get one. So, a Spanish-looking man and a Nordic-looking woman ring my friend Pardon's bell at ten past one in the morning . . .'

As he gruffly told the story, its weak points made themselves apparent.

'The shot wasn't fired in a hotel. Or in the street. So it must have been in an apartment or a house.'

'Do you think they're married?'

'I get the feeling they're not, although I can't say why. If they'd called their usual doctor, assuming they have one, he would have had to report it to the police.'

What intrigued him most was their choice of Pardon, a humble local doctor. Had they picked his name at random out of the telephone book?

'The woman isn't in any of the hospitals or clinics. Pardon offered to lend her one of his wife's bathrobes because her slip and dress were soaked in blood. She preferred to put her clothes back on. Why?'

Lucas opened his mouth, but Maigret had already come up with an answer.

'Because they were planning to make a run for it. I'm not claiming it's a brilliant piece of reasoning, but it stands up.'

'The roads are pretty much impassable. Especially if you've got someone injured in the car.'

'I thought that too. Call Breuker at Orly. If he's not there, get me his idiotic assistant whose name I can never remember.'

Breuker, an Alsatian still who had kept his accent, was head of border police at the airport. He wasn't on duty, and it was his assistant who replied:

'Assistant Chief Inspector Marathieu speaking.'

'Maigret here,' he grunted, irritated by the man's supercilious tone.

'What can I do for you, detective chief inspector?'

'No idea yet. How many international flights have taken off since two, no, two thirty this morning?'

'Only a couple. One for Amsterdam and another for India via Geneva. Departures have been suspended for the last forty minutes because of ice on the runways.'

'Are you far from the car park?'

'Not very, but it's not easy walking outside because of the aforementioned black ice.'

'Would you mind going anyway and seeing if there's a red Alfa Romeo . . .'

'Have you got its number?'

'No. But there can't be that many Alfa Romeos that colour in your car park at this hour of the night. If it's there, ask passport control if they've seen a couple go through answering to this description.'

He repeated what he'd already told Lucas and the other two.

'Call me back at Quai des Orfèvres as soon as you can.'

With a shrug of his shoulders, Maigret turned to the trusty Lucas and added:

'You never know.'

It was a strange investigation, and Maigret seemed not to be taking it entirely seriously, to be approaching it rather like doing a crossword puzzle.

'Marathieu must be fuming,' observed Lucas. 'Imagine sending that stuck-up dandy out into the snow, to skid around on the ice.'

Almost twenty minutes passed before the telephone rang. Maigret announced to no one in particular:

'Assistant Chief Inspector Marathieu speaking . . .'

And those were indeed the first words he heard.

'Well, what about the red car?'

'There's a red Alfa Romeo with Greater Paris number plates in the car park.'

'Locked?'

'Yes. A couple matching the description you gave me took the three ten flight to Amsterdam.'

'Do you have their names?'

'The inspector who checked them off can't remember them. He can only remember the passports. The man had a Colombian passport, and the woman's was Dutch. Both passports had copious visas and stamps.'

'What time are they meant to be landing in Amsterdam?'

'If there aren't any delays and the runway is usable, they'll touch down at four seventeen.'

It was 4.22. The couple were probably showing their passports and going through customs. Anyway, Maigret couldn't take the liberty of contacting the Dutch airport police directly, especially not at this stage in the investigation.

'Well, chief? What do I do?'

'Nothing. Wait to be relieved. I'm going home to bed. Goodnight, boys . . . Actually, can one of you take me home?'

Half an hour later he was fast asleep next to his wife.

2.

Some cases appear dramatic from the outset and immediately make the front pages of all the newspapers. Other
seemingly humdrum ones are only deemed worthy of
three or four lines on the sixth page until it emerges that
a minor news item is really concealing a drama veiled in
mystery.

Maigret was having breakfast, sitting across the table
from his wife by the window. It was eight thirty in the
morning, on such a drab day that they had had to leave
all the lights on. He felt heavy from lack of sleep, his mind
fuddled and full of confused thoughts.

There was still ice in the corners of the windowpanes,
and he thought of how he used to draw pictures or his
initials in it as a child. He remembered the strange feeling,
pleasurable but also slightly painful, when a sliver of ice
worked its way under his fingernails.

After three bitterly cold days, it had started snowing
again, and he could barely make out the houses and lock-
ups on the other side of the street.

'You're not too tired, are you?'

'Another cup of coffee and I'll be just fine.'

In spite of himself he tried to imagine the couple of
elegant foreigners who had suddenly turned up out of the
blue in a humble local doctor's surgery. Pardon had

immediately sensed they were from another world, different to his and Maigret's and to Picpus, the neighbourhood in which they both lived.

Maigret had often been called on to deal with individuals of this sort, people who were equally at home in London, New York and Rome, who took planes the way others took the Métro, who stayed in grand hotels, where they fell in with friends and established routines, whatever the country, and who formed a sort of international freemasonry.

It wasn't just money. It was a certain way of life too, certain attitudes, even a certain morality unlike that of ordinary mortals.

Maigret never felt completely at ease with them and he had trouble suppressing feelings of irritation that might have been taken for jealousy.

'What are you thinking?'

'Nothing.'

He wasn't consciously thinking. Whatever he was doing was too vague for that, and he gave a start when he heard the telephone ring. It was quarter to nine now, and he had been about to get up from the table to put on his overcoat.

'Hello?'

'Lucas here.'

Lucas, who was meant to have come off duty at nine.

'I've just had a call from Chief Inspector Manicle from the fourteenth arrondissement, chief. A man was killed last night in a little town-house on Avenue du Parc-Montsouris. Someone called Nahour, a Lebanese citizen. The cleaner found him when she started work at eight.'

'Has Lapointe got in?'

'I think I can hear him in the corridor. One moment . . . Yes, it's him.'

'Tell him to get a car and come and pick me up. Let Manicle know I'll be there as soon as possible. Then you go and get some sleep.'

'Thanks, chief.'

Maigret repeated in a low voice:

'Nahour . . . Nahour . . .'

Another foreigner. The couple from last night were Dutch and Colombian. Now Nahour and the Middle East.

'A new case?' asked his wife.

'A murder, apparently, on Avenue du Parc-Montsouris.'

He wrapped the thick scarf round his neck, put on his overcoat and grabbed his hat.

'Aren't you going to wait until Lapointe gets here?'

'I need to get some fresh air for a minute.'

Lapointe found him waiting by the kerb. Maigret slid into the front of the little black car.

'Have you got the exact address?'

'Yes, chief. It's the last house before the park, surrounded by a garden. Looks like you didn't get much sleep last night.'

The traffic was slow and heavy. Here and there a car had skidded and was skewed across the road, and pedestrians walked cautiously on the pavements. The Seine was dark green, studded with blocks of ice slowly drifting downstream.

They stopped at a detached house with a mainly glass-fronted ground floor. It looked as if it had been built in

1925 or 1930, when a number of what were then ultramodern houses had sprung up all over Paris, especially Auteuil and Montparnasse.

A policeman pacing up and down outside greeted Maigret, then opened an iron gate leading to a little garden with a bare tree.

The two men followed the path, climbed the four front steps and found another policeman in the hallway who showed them into the studio.

Manicle was in there with one of his inspectors. He was a small, thin man with a moustache, whom Maigret had known for over twenty years. The two men shook hands, then Manicle pointed to a body stretched out behind a mahogany desk.

'The cleaner, a woman called Louise Bodin, rang us at five past eight this morning. She starts work every day at eight. She lives just round the corner in Rue du Saint-Gothard.'

'Who is Nahour?'

'Félix Nahour, forty-two, Lebanese citizen, unemployed. He moved into the house six months ago and rents it furnished from a painter who's in the United States.'

It was very hot in the room despite the huge windows, which were partly covered in frost like the ones at Boulevard Richard-Lenoir.

'Were the curtains open when you got here?'

'No. They were closed. As you can see, they're heavy curtains with a felt lining to keep out the cold.'

'Hasn't the doctor got here?'

'A local doctor came just now and confirmed that he was dead, which was obvious. I've informed the pathologist

28

and I'm expecting him and the prosecutor's office to arrive at any moment.'

Maigret turned to Lapointe.

'Ring Moers then and tell him to come immediately with his men from Criminal Records. No, not from here. There may be prints on the receiver. There'll be a café or public telephone nearby.'

He took off his overcoat and scarf. After an almost sleepless night, the heat was going to his head and making him feel dizzy.

The room was huge. There was a pale-blue carpet on the floor, and the furniture, although not matching, was valuable and in good taste.

Walking round the Empire desk to get a closer look at the dead man, Maigret noticed a photograph in a silver frame by the blotter.

It was a portrait of a young woman with very blonde hair and a sombre smile, who had a three-year-old little girl at her side and a roughly one-year-old baby on her knees.

Frowning, he grabbed the frame to study the image more closely and noticed a two-centimetre-long scar running from her left eye towards her ear.

'Is that his wife?'

'I assume so. I had Records look her up. She is registered under the name of Evelina Nahour, née Wiemers, born in Amsterdam.'

'Is she in the house?'

'No. We knocked on her door. When there was no answer we opened it. The room is in a bit of a mess but the bed hasn't been slept in.'

Maigret bent down over the body, which was curled in a ball so he could only see half the face. As far as he could tell without moving him, a bullet had gone into the man's throat, severing the carotid artery and leaving a vast pool of blood on the carpet.

Nahour was rather small and tubby, with a trim brown moustache. He was going bald. There was a wedding ring on his carefully manicured left hand, and he had tried unsuccessfully to staunch the bleeding with his right.

'Do you know who lived in the house?'

'I've only had the cleaning lady questioned briefly, thinking you'd rather do that. Then I asked the secretary and maid to wait upstairs, where one of my men is making sure they don't talk to each other.'

'Where is this Madame Bodin?'

'In the kitchen. Shall I call her?'

'If you don't mind.'

Lapointe had just come back.

'Done it, chief,' he reported. 'Moers is on his way.'

Louise Bodin came in, her face stubborn and set, a look of defiance in her eyes. Maigret knew the type, the type of most of Paris's cleaners, women who have suffered, been mistreated by life and are now hopelessly anticipating an even grimmer old age. So they become hard and mistrustful and resent the whole world for their misfortunes.

'Are you called Louise Bodin?'

'Madame Bodin, yes.'

She emphasized the 'Madame', which she considered

the last vestige of her dignity as a woman. Her clothes hung off her thin frame, and the look in her dark eyes was so intense they were almost feverish.

'Are you married?'

'I have been.'

'Is your husband dead?'

'He's in Fresnes, if you must know. Good job too.'

Maigret preferred not to ask why her husband had been sent to prison.

'Have you been working in this house for a long time?'

'Five months tomorrow.'

'How did you get the job?'

'I replied to a classified ad. Before that I was doing an hour here, an afternoon or morning there.'

She sniggered, turning to the body, 'Guess what, they put "permanent position" in the ad.'

'You didn't sleep here, did you?'

'No, never. I'd go home at eight at night and I'd come back at eight the next morning.'

'Did Monsieur Nahour work?'

'He must have done something because he had a secretary and he spent hours buried in his papers.'

'Who's his secretary?'

'A guy from his country, Monsieur Fouad.'

'Where is he now?'

She turned to the local chief inspector, then said:

'In his bedroom.'

Her voice had an aggressive edge.

'Don't you like him?'

'Why would I?'

'You got here this morning at eight o'clock. Did you come straight into this room?'

'I went into the kitchen first to heat some water on the gas stove and get my housecoat from the cupboard.'

'Then you opened this door?'

'I always start cleaning in here.'

'When you saw the body, what did you do?'

'I rang the police station.'

'Without telling Monsieur Fouad?'

'Without telling anyone.'

'Why?'

'Because I don't trust people, especially not the ones who live in this house.'

'Why not?'

'Because they're not normal.'

'What do you mean?'

She shrugged and said flatly:

'I know what I mean. No one can stop me thinking my little thoughts, can they?'

'While you were waiting for the police, did you go up and tell the secretary?'

'No. I went and made my coffee in the kitchen. I don't have time to have one at home in the morning.'

'Didn't Monsieur Fouad come downstairs?'

'He hardly ever comes down before ten.'

'Was he asleep?'

'For the second time: I didn't go upstairs.'

'What about the maid?'

'She's Madame's maid. She doesn't look after Monsieur.

Madame used to stay in bed until midday, if not later, so there was nothing to stop her taking liberties.'

'What is she called?'

'Nelly something. I heard her say her surname once or twice but I don't remember it. A Dutch name. She's Dutch, like Madame.'

'Don't you like her either?'

'Is that a crime?'

'I see from this photograph that your employer has two children. Are they in the house?'

'They've never set foot in here.'

'Where do they live?'

'Somewhere on the Côte d'Azur with their nanny.'

'Did their parents go and see them often?'

'I've no idea. They travelled a lot, almost always separately, but I never asked them where they were going.'

The Criminal Records van pulled up in front of the garden, and Moers marched towards the house with his colleagues.

'Did Monsieur Nahour entertain much?'

'What do you mean by entertain?'

'Did he invite friends to lunch or dinner?'

'Not since I've worked here, at any rate. Anyway, he generally had dinner in town.'

'What about his wife?'

'She did too.'

'Together?'

'I never followed them.'

'Visitors?'

'Monsieur would sometimes see people in his office.'

'Friends?'

'I don't listen at doors. They were almost always foreigners, people from his country, who he spoke to in a language I didn't understand.'

'Was Monsieur Fouad present at these discussions?'

'Sometimes he was, sometimes he wasn't.'

'One moment, Moers. You can't start before the pathologist gets here. Thank you, Madame Bodin. Please stay in the kitchen and don't do any housework until the premises have been inspected. Where is Madame Nahour's bedroom?'

'Upstairs, on the first floor.'

'Did Monsieur Nahour and his wife share a bedroom?'

'No. Monsieur's apartment is on the ground floor, across the corridor.'

'Isn't there a dining room?'

'The studio was used as a dining room.'

'Thank you for your cooperation.'

'Don't mention it,' she said, before making a dignified exit.

Moments later Maigret was climbing the stairs, which were carpeted in the same lavender-blue as the studio. Manicle and Lapointe tagged along. On the first-floor landing they found a local inspector in plain clothes who was smoking a cigarette with an air of resignation.

'Madame Nahour's bedroom?'

'That one, straight across.'

The room was spacious and furnished in the Louis XVI style. The bed may not have been slept in, but the general impression was still one of mess. A green dress and some underwear were scattered on the carpet. The wardrobe doors were wide open, suggesting a hurried departure. Coat hangers were lying around, one on the bed and another on a silk-covered armchair, as if someone had been grabbing clothes and stuffing them into a suitcase.

Maigret idly opened a few drawers.

'Will you call the maid, Lapointe?'

This took a while. They stood around for several minutes, and only then did a young woman, who was almost as blonde as Madame Nahour, with strikingly pale-blue eyes, appear in the doorway, followed by Lapointe.

She wasn't wearing a work smock or the traditional black dress and white apron but a noticeably close-fitting tweed suit.

She looked like the Dutch girls on cocoa tins, and the only thing missing was her national bonnet with its two wings.

'Come in. Sit down.'

Her face remained expressionless, as if she hadn't grasped what was happening or who these people standing in front of her were.

'What's your name?'

She shook her head, but opened her mouth enough to mutter:

'No understand.'

'Can't you speak French?'

She motioned that she couldn't.

'Just Dutch?'

Maigret was already envisaging the difficulties of finding a translator.

'English too.'

'You speak English?'

'Yes.'

The little English Maigret spoke was not going to be enough to question what might be an important witness.

'Do you want me to translate, chief?' Lapointe offered shyly.

Maigret looked at him in surprise; the young inspector had never told him he spoke English.

'Where did you learn?'

'I've been studying it every day for a year.'

The young girl looked at them in turn. When they asked her a question she didn't answer immediately but waited until she had digested what had been said to her.

She didn't seem hostile and suspicious, like the cleaner, but somehow impassive, either from birth or because she had picked it up at some stage in her life. Was she putting it on deliberately, to seem of less than average intelligence?

Even when translated into English, their questions only seemed to reach her brain with difficulty, and her answers were brief, rudimentary.

She was called Velthuis and was twenty-four years old. She was from Friesland, in the north of the Netherlands and had moved to Amsterdam when she was fifteen.

'Did she start working for Madame Nahour straight away?'

Lapointe translated the question and in reply only got the word:

'No.'

'When did she become her maid?'

'Six years ago.'

'How?'

'Through an advert in an Amsterdam newspaper.'

'Was Madame Nahour already married?'

'Yes.'

'Since when?'

'She doesn't know.'

Maigret was having a hard time remaining calm. With these short yes and no answers, the questioning could take hours.

'Tell her I don't like being taken for a fool.'

Lapointe translated in an embarrassed voice. The young girl glanced at Maigret with slight surprise before resuming her look of total indifference.

Two dark-coloured cars pulled up by the kerb, and Maigret grunted:

'The prosecutor's office. Stay with her, will you? Try to get as much out of her as you can.'

Noiret, the deputy prosecutor, was a middle-aged man with an old-fashioned grey goatee, who after doing the rounds of most of the provincial courts had finally been appointed to Paris, where he was scrupulously avoiding complications as he counted the days to his retirement.

The forensic pathologist, a man called Colinet, was bent over the body. It was a while now since he had replaced Dr Paul, whom Maigret had worked with for so many years.

37

Others had similarly disappeared over the years: Coméliau, for instance, the examining magistrate whom Maigret could have called his close personal enemy and missed occasionally.

Cayotte, the relatively young examining magistrate in charge of this case, made a point of letting the police work on their own for two or three days before he got involved in an investigation.

The doctor had changed the position of the body twice, and his hands were sticky with congealed blood. He looked around for Maigret.

'Naturally I can't tell you anything conclusive before the post-mortem. The bullet's entrance wound, here, makes me think we're dealing with a medium- or large-calibre weapon, and that the shot was fired from more than two metres away.

'The lack of an exit wound means the bullet is still in the body. I can't really see it coming to rest in the throat, which wouldn't offer sufficient resistance, so I suppose that, fired more or less upwards from a low position, it lodged in the skull.'

'Do you mean the victim was standing while the murderer was sitting down – on the other side of the desk, for instance?'

'Not necessarily sitting, he could have fired without raising his arm, from the hip.'

It was only when the ambulance men lifted the body to put it on a stretcher that a 6.35 calibre pearl-handled automatic became visible on the carpet.

The deputy prosecutor and examining magistrate looked at Maigret to see what he made of it.

'I assume the wound couldn't have been caused by that gun?' Maigret asked the pathologist.

'That's my opinion, at least for the moment.'

'Moers, will you examine the pistol?'

Grabbing a cloth, Moers picked up the gun, sniffed it, then took out the magazine.

'A bullet's missing, chief.'

Now the body was being taken away, the men from Criminal Records could set to work, and the photographer could start. He had already taken some photographs of the dead man. Everyone came and went. Little groups formed. Noiret, the deputy prosecutor, tugged at Maigret's sleeve.

'What nationality do you think he is?'

'Lebanese.'

'Do you think it's a political crime?'

The prospect terrified him, because he remembered similar cases that had proved disastrous for most of the people involved.

'I think I'll be able to answer that pretty quickly.'

'Have you questioned the staff?'

'The cleaner, who is not very forthcoming, and I've started with the maid, who's even less. She doesn't seem to speak a word of French, though, it's true. Inspector Lapointe is questioning her in English upstairs at the minute.'

'Let me know as soon as you can.'

He looked around for the examining magistrate so they could leave. Today's visit from the prosecutor's office was merely a formality.

'Do you need me or my men any more?' asked the local chief inspector.

'You're free to go, my friend, but it would be a help if you left your inspectors a while longer, as well as the officer on guard at the door.'

'Whatever you need.'

The living room gradually emptied out, and at one point Maigret found himself standing in front of a bookcase containing over 300 books. He was surprised to see that they were almost all scientific works, mostly mathematics, and a whole row, in French and English, were devoted to probability theory.

Opening the cupboards under the shelves, he found stacks of sheets of paper, some mimeographed, containing nothing but columns of numbers.

'Let's talk again before you leave, Moers . . . And send the gun to Gastinne-Renette for tests . . . Actually, put this in as well.'

He reached into his pocket for the bullet Pardon had given him, which was wrapped in a piece of cotton.

'Where did you find it?'

'I'll tell you later. I need to know urgently whether it came from this gun.'

He lit his pipe as he climbed the stairs and glanced into the room where Lapointe and the young Dutch woman were sitting facing one another. The inspector was taking notes in a notebook, using the dressing table as a desk.

'Where's the secretary?' he asked the local inspector who was standing around looking bored in the corridor.

'The door at the end.'

'Has he been complaining?'

'He opens his door now and then to have a listen. He had a telephone call.'

'What did the chief inspector say to him this morning?'

'That his boss had been murdered and that he was to stay in his room until told otherwise.'

'Were you there?'

'Yes.'

'Did he seem surprised?'

'He's not the sort to show his feelings. You'll see.'

Maigret knocked at the same time as he turned the handle and pushed open the door. The room was neat, the bed carefully made, despite having been slept in the previous night. There was nothing on the floor. A little desk stood in front of the window with a tan leather armchair beside it, and a man was sitting in the armchair, watching Maigret coming towards him.

It was difficult to tell his age. He was dark, very Arab-looking, and, although lined, his face could just as easily have been that of a forty-year-old as a sixty-year-old. His thick, bushy hair was jet black, without a speck of white.

He did not get up, offered no form of greeting, merely looked at his visitor with his smouldering eyes, his features displaying no discernible emotion.

'I imagine you speak French?'

A nod.

'Detective Chief Inspector Maigret, head of the Crime Squad. I assume you are Monsieur Nahour's secretary?'

Another nod.

'May I ask you your full name?'

'Fouad Ouéni.'

His voice was muffled, as if he were suffering from chronic laryngitis.

'Do you know what happened last night in the studio?'

'No.'

'But you've been told that Monsieur Nahour has been killed, haven't you?'

'That's all.'

'Where were you?'

Not a flicker of response. Maigret had rarely come across such a lack of cooperation as he had since entering this house. The cleaner only answered questions in a hostile, evasive manner. The Dutch maid was monosyllabic.

And now Fouad Ouéni, who was wearing an immaculate black suit, white shirt and dark-grey tie, was responding to Maigret with total indifference, if not contempt.

'Did you spend last night in this room?'

'From one thirty in the morning.'

'You mean you got back at one thirty in the morning?'

'I thought you'd gathered that.'

'Where were you until then?'

'At the Saint-Michel Club.'

'A gambling club?'

The man shrugged.

'Where is it exactly?'

'Above the Bar des Tilleuls.'

'Did you gamble?'

'No.'

'What did you do?'

'Wrote down the winning numbers.'

It must have been the sarcasm that made him seem so pleased with himself. Maigret sat down on a chair and continued with his questions, as if he was oblivious to the hostility of the person facing him.

'When you came back were there any lights on in the studio?'

'I don't know.'

'Were the curtains drawn?'

'I suppose so. They were every evening.'

'Did you see any light under the door?'

'You never see any light under the door.'

'Was Monsieur Nahour generally in bed by then?'

'It depended.'

'On what?'

'On him.'

'Did he often go out in the evening?'

'When he felt like it.'

'Where did he go?'

'Wherever he wanted.'

'On his own?'

'He'd leave the house on his own.'

'Did he take the car?'

'He'd call a taxi.'

'Didn't he drive?'

'He didn't like driving. I was his chauffeur during the day.'

'What sort of car did he have?'

'A Bentley.'

'Is it in the garage?'

'I haven't checked. I haven't been allowed out of my room.'

'What about Madame Nahour?'

'What do you want to know?'

'Has she got a car too?'

'A green Triumph.'

'Did she go out yesterday evening?'

'I never had anything to do with her.'

'What time did you leave the house?'

'Ten thirty.'

'Was she here?'

'I don't know.'

'What about Monsieur Nahour?'

'I don't know if he'd got back. He must have had dinner in town.'

'Do you know where?'

'Probably at the Petit Beyrouth, his usual place.'

'Who did the cooking in the house?'

'No one in particular.'

'Breakfast?'

'I made Monsieur Félix's.'

'Who is Monsieur Félix?'

'Monsieur Nahour.'

'Why do you call him Monsieur Félix?'

'Because there's Monsieur Maurice too.'

'Who's Monsieur Maurice?'

'Monsieur Nahour's father.'

'Does he live here?'

'No. Lebanon.'

'Who else?'

'Monsieur Pierre, Monsieur Félix's brother.'

'Who lives where?'

'Geneva.'

'Who called you this morning?'

'No one called me.'

'But the telephone was heard ringing in your room.'

'I asked to speak to Geneva and they called me back when they got through.'

'Monsieur Pierre?'

'Yes.'

'Did you inform him?'

'I told him Monsieur Félix was dead. Monsieur Pierre will be at Orly in a few minutes, he took the first plane.'

'Do you know what he does in Geneva?'

'Banker.'

'And Monsieur Maurice Nahour in Beirut?'

'Banker.'

'And Monsieur Félix?'

'He didn't have a job.'

'Had you worked for him for a long time?'

'I didn't work for him.'

'Didn't you carry out the duties of a secretary? You said just now that you made his breakfast and drove for him.'

'I helped him.'

'Had you done so for a long time?'

'Eighteen years.'

'Did you know him back in Beirut?'

'I met him at Law School.'

'In Paris?'

He nodded, stiff and impassive in his armchair. Maigret felt himself losing patience.

'Did he have enemies?'

'Not that I know of.'

'Was he involved in politics?'

'Definitely not.'

'So you went out around ten thirty without knowing who was or wasn't in the house. You went to a gambling club on Boulevard Saint-Michel, where you noted the winning numbers but didn't gamble. Then you came back at one thirty and came up here, still not knowing anybody's whereabouts. Is that right? You didn't see anything or hear anything, and the last thing you were expecting was to be woken up with the news that Monsieur Nahour had been shot dead.'

'Nobody's said anything about him being shot.'

'What do you know about Félix Nahour's family life?'

'Nothing. It's none of my concern.'

'Was it a happy marriage?'

'I don't know.'

'I get the impression from what you've said that the husband and wife rarely spent time together.'

'That's quite common, I think.'

'Why don't the children live in Paris?'

'Perhaps the Côte d'Azur suits them better.'

'Where did Monsieur Nahour live before renting this house?'

'All over the place. In Italy. In Cuba for a year, before the revolution. We also had a villa at Deauville.'

'Do you often go to the Saint-Michel?'

'Two or three times a week.'

'And you never gamble?'

'Hardly ever.'

'Will you come downstairs with me?'

They made for the stairs. Fouad Ouéni looked even thinner and leaner when he stood up.

'How old are you?'

'I don't know. There wasn't a registry office in the mountains when I was born. My passport says I'm fifty-one.'

'Are you older or younger?'

'I don't know.'

In the studio Moers' men were putting their equipment back in its boxes.

When the van had driven off and the two men were left alone, Maigret asked, 'Look around and tell me if anything's missing. Or if there's something that wasn't here before.'

Ouéni tore himself away from studying the pool of blood and opened the right-hand drawer of the desk.

'The automatic has gone,' he observed.

'What sort of gun is it?'

'A Browning 6.35.'

'Pearl-handled?'

'Yes.'

'Why did Félix Nahour have what's generally considered a woman's gun?'

'It was Madame Nahour's before.'

'How many years ago?'

'I don't know.'

'Did he take it off her?'

'He didn't say.'

'Did he have a licence to carry firearms?'

'He never carried that pistol.'

Considering the subject closed, the Lebanese man

looked through the rest of the desk drawers, which contained an assortment of files, then went over to the bookshelves and opened the cupboards beneath them.

'Could you tell me what those lists of figures are?'

Ouéni looked at him with a mixture of surprise and sarcasm, as if Maigret should have worked it out for himself.

'They're the winning numbers in the major casinos. Agencies send out the mimeographed lists to their subscribers. Monsieur Félix got the others from a casino employee.'

Maigret was going to ask another question, but Lapointe appeared in the doorway.

'Will you come upstairs for a minute, chief?'

'Progress?'

'Not really, but I think I should bring you up to date.'

'I must ask you not to leave the house without my permission, Monsieur Ouéni.'

'Can I go and make myself a cup of coffee?'

Maigret turned his back on him with a shrug.

3.

Maigret had rarely felt so disorientated, so far from normal life, beset by that feeling of unease that comes over you in dreams when the ground gives way under your feet.

The few passers-by in the snow-covered streets concentrated on staying on their feet, the cars, taxis and buses drove slowly, and everywhere sand and salt trucks crawled along the pavements.

Electric lights burned in almost every window, and snow still fell from a slate-grey sky.

He could have guessed what was going on in all these boxy little dwellings filled with living, breathing human beings. For over thirty years, he had got to know Paris neighbourhood by neighbourhood, street by street, and yet here he felt immersed in a different world, where he couldn't predict how anyone would react.

What sort of life had Félix Nahour been leading until a few hours ago? What exactly was his relationship with his secretary – secretary in everything but name – and wife and two children? Why were the children on the Côte d'Azur, why . . .

There were so many whys that he couldn't address them individually. Nothing was straightforward or clear-cut. Nothing was the way it was in other families, other households.

Pardon had felt a similar unease last night when a couple of strangers had burst into his local doctor's surgery.

The story of a shot fired from a moving car was hard to credit, as was the old woman who pointed out the doctor's building.

Félix Nahour with his works on mathematics and his lists of winning and losing numbers in various casinos did not fit into any category Maigret knew of, and Fouad Ouéni was from an equally unfamiliar world.

Everything here seemed to be fake and everyone seemed to be lying, an intuition that Lapointe confirmed as they went upstairs.

'I wonder if this girl's completely normal, chief. Judging by her answers, when she agrees to give any that is, and the way she looks at me, she seems to have the naivety and mentality of a ten-year-old, but I wonder if it isn't all a trick or a game.'

As they went into Madame Nahour's bedroom, where Nelly was still sitting in a silk-covered chair, Lapointe remarked:

'Incidentally, chief, the children aren't the age they were when the photo was taken. The girl's five now, and the little boy is two.'

'Do you know where they're living with the nanny?'

'In Mougins, in a hotel called the Pension des Palmiers.'

'Have they been there long?'

'As far as I can work out, the boy was born in Cannes and has never been to Paris.'

The maid was looking at them with her clear, pale eyes, apparently not understanding a word they were saying.

'I've found other photographs in a drawer she showed me. A dozen snaps of the children as babies, then walking, then there's this one, on a beach, of Nahour and his wife when she was young, probably when they first met. And, last one, here's a photo of Madame Nahour with a female friend by a canal in Amsterdam.'

The friend was ugly, with a flat nose and poky little eyes, but nevertheless she had a likeable, open face.

'The only letters I've found in the room are from a girl in Dutch. They cover a period of about seven years, and the last one was written about a fortnight ago.'

'Has Nelly ever gone to the Netherlands with her employer?'

'She says not.'

'Does she go there often?'

'Occasionally. By herself, apparently. But I'm not sure that Nelly completely understands the questions I ask her, even in English.'

'Find a translator for these letters. What does she say about yesterday evening and night?'

'Nothing. She doesn't know anything. The house isn't that big, and yet everyone seems in the dark about what the others are doing. She thinks that Madame Nahour had dinner in town.'

'Alone? Didn't anyone come and pick her up? She didn't order a taxi.'

'She says she doesn't know.'

'Didn't she help Madame Nahour dress?'

'I asked her that, and she says no one rang for her. She ate in the kitchen, as usual, then went up to her room, read a Dutch newspaper and went to bed. She showed me the newspaper, which is from the day before yesterday.'

'Didn't she hear any footsteps in the corridor?'

'She wasn't paying attention. Once she falls asleep apparently nothing can wake her.'

'What time does she start in the morning?'

'There's no set time.'

Maigret was vainly trying to work out what was going on behind the ivory-smooth forehead of the maid, who was smiling vaguely at him.

'Tell her she can go and have her breakfast but that she is not allowed to leave the house.'

When Lapointe had translated these instructions, Nelly stood up, gave a little curtsey like a girl at a boarding school and headed calmly for the stairs.

'She's lying, chief.'

'How do you know?'

'She says she didn't come into this room last night. And the local police stopped her leaving her room this morning. But when I asked her what coat her employer was wearing, she answered without a moment's hesitation:

' "The sealskin one . . ."'

'Well, the cupboards were closed, and in one of them I found a mink coat and a grey astrakhan in the other.'

'I want you to take the car and go to Doctor Pardon's on Boulevard Voltaire. Show him the photograph on the desk downstairs.'

There was a telephone in the bedroom. When it started ringing, Maigret picked it up and heard two voices, the pathologist's and Ouéni's.

'Yes,' the latter was saying. 'He's still here. Wait, I'll let him know . . .'

'There's no need, Monsieur Ouéni,' Maigret put in. 'Will you hang up, please?'

So the three telephones in the house, including the secretary's, were on the same line.

'Hello, this is Maigret.'

'Colinet here. I've only just started the post-mortem, but I thought you'd like to know the first finding right away. It wasn't suicide.'

'I never thought it was.'

'Nor did I, but now we know for certain. I'm not a ballistics expert but I'm still confident that the bullet I found in the skull, as I'd expected, was fired by a medium- or large-calibre gun, a 7.32 or .45. I'd say it was fired from between three and four metres away, and the skull has been split.'

'Time of death?'

'To establish that more exactly, I'll need to know the time he had dinner and then run tests on his intestines.'

'At a rough guess?'

'Around midnight.'

'Thank you, doctor.'

Lapointe had left, and his car could be heard turning into the avenue.

There were two men downstairs talking in a foreign language, which Maigret eventually recognized as Arabic. He went down and found Ouéni talking to a stranger in the corridor, as the local inspector looked on, not daring to say anything.

The newcomer looked like a slightly older, thinner version of Félix Nahour. He was taller as well, and his dark hair was greying at the temples.

'Monsieur Pierre Nahour?'

'Are you the police?' the man asked suspiciously.

'Detective Chief Inspector Maigret, head of the Crime Squad.'

'What has happened to my brother? Where is his body?'

'He was killed last night by a gunshot wound to the throat, and his body has been taken to the Forensic Institute.'

'Can I see him?'

'In a moment.'

'Why not now?'

'Because the post-mortem is being performed. Come in, Monsieur Nahour.'

He wondered for a moment whether to ask Ouéni into the office as well but decided against it.

'Would you go and wait in your room?'

Ouéni and Nahour exchanged glances; Maigret didn't see any fondness for the secretary in the newcomer's eyes.

Once the door was shut, the banker from Geneva asked:

'Did it happen in here?'

Maigret pointed to the large bloodstain on the carpet. The man was lost in thought for a moment, as he would have been if he were standing in front of the body.

'How did it happen?'

'No one knows. Apparently he had dinner in town, and that was the last anyone saw of him.'

'Lina?'

'Do you mean Madame Nahour? Her maid claims that she also went out for dinner and didn't come back.'

'Isn't she here?'

'Her bed hasn't been slept in, and she's taken her luggage.'

Pierre Nahour did not seem surprised.

'Ouéni?'

'He apparently went to a gambling club on Boulevard Saint-Michel and noted the winning numbers until one in the morning. When he came back, he didn't try to find out if his employer was in the house or not and went up to bed. He didn't hear anything . . .'

They were sitting facing one another. The banker had automatically taken a cigar out of his pocket but was hesitating to light it, perhaps out of a sort of respect for the deceased, even though the body was no longer there.

'I have to ask you some questions, Monsieur Nahour, I apologize if they seem intrusive. Were you on good terms with your brother?'

'On very good terms, although we didn't see each other often.'

'Why?'

'Because I live in Geneva and, when I do travel, I generally go to Lebanon. My brother had no call to come to Geneva. It wasn't one of his stamping grounds.'

'Ouéni has told me that Félix Nahour didn't have a job.'

'That's true to a degree. I think, Monsieur Maigret, that rather than wait for your questions, I should fill you in on various things that will help you to understand the situation. My father was, and still is, a banker in Beirut. His bank started out as a very small concern, mainly intended to finance imports and exports, since Beirut is the gateway for trade with the Middle East. Beirut has the most banks, per capita, of anywhere in the world.'

He finally decided to light his cigar. His hands were as carefully manicured as his brother's, and he was wearing a wedding ring as well.

'We are Maronite Christians, hence our first names. My father's business grew over the years, and he now runs one of the largest banks in Lebanon.

'I studied at the Law Faculty in Paris and then the Institute of Comparative Law.'

'Before your brother arrived?'

'He is five years younger than me, so I have a head start. When he got here I'd almost finished my studies.'

'Did you move to Geneva straight away?'

'I worked with my father at first, then we decided to open a branch in Switzerland, the Comptoir Libanais, which I run. It is a fairly small operation with five employees and an office on the second floor of a building in Avenue du Rhône.'

Now that he was dealing with someone who spoke to him with at least a semblance of clarity, Maigret tried to fit the protagonists into place.

'Do you have other brothers?'

'Only a sister, whose husband runs another branch like mine in Istanbul.'

'So you, your father and your brother-in-law control a large part of Lebanon's trade?'

'Say a quarter, or if we're being more modest, a fifth.'

'And your brother Félix wasn't involved in the family business?'

'He was the youngest. He started studying law too, but his heart wasn't in it, and he spent most of his time in the back rooms of the bars in the Latin Quarter. He had discovered poker, at which he turned out to be very good, and he'd play all night.'

'Is that when he met Ouéni?'

'I'm not saying Ouéni, who's Muslim rather than Maronite, was his evil genius, but I'm not far off thinking so. Ouéni was very poor, like most people from the mountains. He had to work his way through university.'

'If I understand correctly, judging by various things I found in this office, your brother became a professional gambler.'

'In so far as one can call it a profession. One day we heard he'd dropped out of law to study mathematics at the Sorbonne. He and my father fell out for a number of years.'

'What about you?'

'I'd see him from time to time. I had to lend him money to begin with.'

'Which he paid back?'

'In full. You mustn't think after what I've just said that my brother was a failure. The first months or couple of years were difficult, but it wasn't long before he was winning large sums of money, and I'm sure he had become richer than me.'

'Did he and your father patch things up?'

'Pretty quickly. We Maronites have a strong sense of family.'

57

'I imagine your brother played mostly in casinos?'

'At Deauville, Cannes, Evian, Enghien in the winter. For a year or two before Castro he was a technical adviser and, I think, associate of the casino in Havana. He didn't gamble haphazardly, he put his maths studies to good use.'

'Are you married, Monsieur Nahour?'

'Married with four children, one of whom is twenty-two and studying at Harvard.'

'When did your brother get married?'

'Wait . . . It was the year of . . . Seven years ago.'

'Do you know his wife?'

'Naturally I've made Lina's acquaintance.'

'Did you meet her before the marriage?'

'No. We all thought my brother was a confirmed bachelor.'

'How did you find out about the wedding?'

'By letter.'

'Do you know where it took place?'

'In Trouville, where Félix had rented a summer house . . .'

Pierre Nahour's face had clouded over a little.

'What sort of woman is she?'

'I don't know how to answer that.'

'Why?'

'Because I've only met her twice.'

'Did your brother go to Geneva to introduce her to you?'

'No. I came to Paris on business and I met up with them both at the Ritz, where they were living at the time.'

'Didn't your brother ever go to Lebanon with her?'

'No. My father saw them a few months later at Evian, where he had gone to take the waters.'

'Did your father approve of the marriage?'

'It is hard for me to speak for my father.'

'What about you?'

'It was none of my business.'

They were lapsing back into haziness, into vague or ambiguous answers.

'Do you know where your brother met the woman who was to become his wife?'

'He never told me but it was easy to work it out. The year before they got married, the Miss Europe contest was held at Deauville. Félix was there because they played for very high stakes at the casino and the house lost almost every night. The crown went to a nineteen-year-old Dutch woman, Lina Wiemers.'

'Whom your brother married.'

'About a year later. In the meantime the two of them travelled around a lot, or more precisely, the three of them, because Félix never went anywhere without Fouad Ouéni.'

They were interrupted by the telephone. Maigret picked up. Lapointe was on the other end of the line.

'I'm calling from Doctor Pardon's, chief. He recognized the photograph immediately. It's the injured woman he treated last night.'

'Right. Come back here, will you? Drop in at headquarters first and ask Janvier, if he's there – or Torrence or somebody else if he's not – to bring a car and meet me at Avenue du Parc-Montsouris.'

He hung up.

'I'm sorry, Monsieur Nahour. I have an even more

indiscreet question to ask – you'll understand why in a minute. Do you know if your brother and his wife got on well?'

The man's face seemed to close.

'I'm sorry, I can't enlighten you on that subject. I have never concerned myself with my brother's married life.'

'His room was on the ground floor, and his wife's on the first floor. As far as I can tell from the extremely grudging witness statements I've secured so far, they didn't eat together and rarely went out as a couple.'

Pierre Nahour didn't flinch, but his cheeks reddened.

'The extent of the staff in this house is a cleaner, Fouad Ouéni, whose role is fairly indeterminate, and a Dutch maid, who only speaks her native language and English.'

'Besides Arabic, my brother spoke French, English, Spanish and Italian, as well as some German.'

'Ouéni made his master's breakfast, and Nelly Velthuis her mistress's. Lunch was the same, when they ate it here, and they mostly went out for dinner, but to separate restaurants.'

'I wasn't aware of that.'

'Where are your children, Monsieur Nahour?'

'Well . . . In Geneva, of course. Or more precisely, eight kilometres outside Geneva, where we have our house.'

'Your brother's children live on the Côte d'Azur with a nanny.'

'Félix often went to see them and he spent part of the year in Cannes.'

'What about his wife?'

'I imagine she went to see them too.'

'Did you ever hear talk of her having a lover or lovers?'

'We don't move in the same circles.'

'I'm going to try to piece together the events of last night for you, Monsieur Nahour, at least as much of them as we know. At some point before one in the morning your brother was hit in the throat by a bullet fired by a large-calibre automatic, the type and probably the make of which we will know when we receive the firearms expert's report. When this happened, he was standing behind his desk . . .

'Now, your brother, like his attacker, was holding a gun, a pearl-handled 6.35 pistol, which was usually kept in the right-hand drawer of his desk which we found half-open . . .

'I don't know how many people were in the room, but we are certain that your sister-in-law was present.'

'How can you know that?'

'Because she was wounded by a bullet fired from the 6.35. Have you ever heard of a doctor called Doctor Pardon, who lives on Boulevard Voltaire?'

'I'm not familiar with the neighbourhood and I've never heard that name.'

'Your sister-in-law must have known him, or the man with her.'

'You mean there was another man in this studio?'

'I can't say for sure. Madame Nahour, before or after these events, hurriedly crammed some clothes and under-wear into one or more suitcases. Soon afterwards, dressed in a sealskin coat, she and her friend got out of a red Alfa Romeo outside 76a, Boulevard Voltaire and rang the doctor's bell.'

'Who was the man?'

'All we know is that he's a twenty-five- or twenty-six-year-old Colombian citizen.'

Pierre Nahour didn't flinch, or even start.

'You have no idea who he might be?' asked Maigret, looking him in the eye.

'None,' he said flatly, taking his cigar out of his mouth.

'Your sister-in-law was wounded in the back, not very seriously though. Doctor Pardon treated her. The Colombian told an outlandish story whereby the woman, whom he didn't know, was shot metres away from him by one or more individuals ostensibly firing out of a car window.'

'Where is she now?'

'Most probably in Amsterdam. As the doctor was washing his hands and taking off his bloodstained coat, the couple silently left his office. Next thing we know they're at Orly, where the red car still is. Two passengers, Dutch and Colombian, answering to their description, boarded the flight for Amsterdam.'

Maigret stood up and went to empty his pipe in the ashtray before filling another one that he took out of his pocket.

'I've put my cards on the table, Monsieur Nahour. I expect you to be equally frank in return. I am going back to my office at Quai des Orfèvres. One of my inspectors will remain in the house and ensure that the cleaner, Ouéni and Nelly don't go anywhere without my permission.'

'What about me?'

'I'd like you to stay here too, because, once the post-mortem is finished, I am going to ask you to come and identify the body. It's just a formality, but an indispensable one.'

He went and planted himself in front of the bay window. The snow had let up, but the sky wasn't any brighter. Two of the Police Judiciaire's little black cars were parked by the kerb, and Lapointe was getting out of one, Janvier out of another. Both of them crossed the garden, and the door could be heard opening on to the hallway.

'Perhaps the next time we see each other, Monsieur Nahour, you will be able to tell me more about your sister-in-law's relationship with your brother and, possibly, with other men.'

Without responding, Pierre Nahour watched him leave in silence.

'You stay here, Lapointe. I'm going to headquarters with Janvier.'

And with that Maigret wrapped the thick scarf round his neck and put on his overcoat.

It was 11.50 a.m. when Maigret, leaning back in his chair, finally got through to Amsterdam.

'Keulemans? Hello, Maigret here, calling from Paris . . .'

The head of Amsterdam's Crime Squad, Jef Keulemans, was still young, hardly forty, with a willowy boyish frame, pink cheeks and blond hair that made him look ten years younger.

When he had come to Paris on a work placement, Maigret had shown him the ropes at the Police Judiciaire. The two men had become good friends and saw each other every now and then at international congresses.

'Very well, Keulemans, thank you . . . My wife too, yes . . . What? The harbour is frozen over? If it's any consolation, Paris has become a skating rink, and now it's started snowing again.

'Hello . . . Listen, I've got a favour to ask you. I'm sorry that's why I'm calling. All unofficial, of course. I haven't got time to fill in the paperwork I need to go through the official channels, for one thing. And I don't have enough facts to hand either.

'Last night, two people I'm interested in arrived on a KLM flight from Orly that left around three in the morning. A man and a woman. They may have pretended not to be together. The man, who has a Colombian passport, is around twenty-five. The woman, Dutch by birth, is called Evelina Nahour, née Wiemers, and sometimes stays for brief periods in Amsterdam, where she grew up.

'I imagine they both filled out landing cards, which you'll be able to find at the airport . . .

'Madame Nahour doesn't live in Holland, but she has a friend in Amsterdam, Anna Keegel, who puts a Lomanstraat address on the back of her letters. Do you know it?

'Good . . . No, no need to arrest them. Perhaps if you find Madame Nahour, you could just tell her that her husband is dead and that they're expecting her for the reading of the will. Tell her her brother-in-law has come to Paris too. Don't mention the police.

'Nahour has been murdered, yes . . . Shot in the throat . . .

What? . . . She probably knows but she may not conceivably. Nothing would surprise me in this business.

'I don't want her frightened off. If she is still with her travelling companion, don't bother him. If they've split up, I imagine she'll telephone him to tell him about your visit . . .

'That's kind of you, Keulemans . . . I'm going home to have lunch and I'll expect a call this afternoon . . . Thank you.'

He took advantage of the direct line to dial his own number.

'What's for lunch?' he asked as soon as his wife came on.

'I've made sauerkraut, which I was pretty sure I was going to have to reheat this evening, if not tomorrow.'

'I'll be home in half an hour.'

He chose one of the pipes from the row on his desk and filled it as he walked slowly down the corridor. When he was almost at the end, he knocked on the door of Detective Chief Inspector Lardois, head of the Gambling Squad. Lardois had joined the Police Judiciaire at pretty much the same time as him, and the two men had been on first-name terms from the outset.

'Morning, Raoul.'

'What's reminded you of my existence? Our offices are twenty metres apart, and you only visit me once a year, if that.'

'I could say the same to you.'

This didn't prevent them seeing each other every morning at the daily briefing in the commissioner's office, although on a more official footing, it was true.

'You'll think my questions naive, but I haven't a clue about gambling, I freely admit it. First, is there really such a thing as a professional gambler?'

'Casino managers are professionals really, because, when it comes down to it, they're gambling against the customers . . . When the house is banker on two tables, they'll sometimes go halves with a gambling expert or a syndicate. That's it, as far as well-established pros are concerned.

'Then there are the people, not many, it has to be said, who live off gambling for varying periods of time, either because they have exceptional luck or because they have considerable financial resources and are especially smart.'

'Can you gamble scientifically?'

'Apparently. Some gamblers, again very few, can make complicated calculations of probability between the deal and choice of card.'

'Have you heard of someone called Félix Nahour?'

'Every croupier in France and beyond knows him. He falls into the second category, although for a while he was a baccarat banker with an American syndicate in Havana.'

'Is he honest?'

'If he wasn't, he would have got a record a long time ago and be barred from the gaming rooms. You only find sleazy little cardsharps occasionally in the smaller casinos, and anyway they soon get caught.'

'What do you know about Nahour?'

'For a start that he has a very beautiful wife, a Miss some place or other, whom I met several times in Cannes and Biarritz. Then that at some point he worked with a group from the Middle East.'

'A gambling syndicate?'

'If you like. Let's call it a group of gamblers who can't or won't play themselves. If a pro is going to take on the house at Cannes or Deauville, for instance, he needs to have enough millions to stay the course until his own luck turns. In other words, he has to be on an equal footing with the casinos, which have virtually inexhaustible funds.

'Hence the creation of syndicates, which operate like finance companies, except they work more discreetly.

'For a long time a South American syndicate used to send an operative to Deauville every year, and on a number of occasions the house found itself in a tight corner.'

'Has Nahour always been backed by a syndicate?'

'People say he goes it alone these days, but it's impossible to check.'

'Another question. Do you know the Saint-Michel Club?'

Lardois hesitated before answering.

'Yes. I've raided it two or three times.'

'Why's it still going, then?'

'You're not going to tell me Nahour gambles there, are you?'

'No, but his secretary, or assistant, spends a good part of the night there two or three times a week.'

'Special Branch asked me to turn a blind eye. A lot of the club's clientele are from the Middle East and live in that neighbourhood. It's a good place to keep an eye on them and our colleague is no slouch. Has there been a fight?'

'No.'

'Something else?'

'No.'

'Is Nahour involved in a case?'

'He was murdered last night.'

'In a club?'

'At his home.'

'Are you going to tell me what happened?'

'As soon as I know myself.'

Twenty minutes later, Maigret was sitting across the dining table from his wife, enjoying a delicious Alsatian sauerkraut of a kind you'll only find in two restaurants in Paris. The salt pork was particularly flavourful, as the critics would say, and he had opened some bottles of Strasbourg beer.

The snow was still falling outside the window, and it was good to be in the snug, not have to venture out on pavements as slippery as Amsterdam's harbour.

'Tired?'

'Not too bad.'

After a silence, with a slightly sardonic look at his wife, he added:

'Policemen shouldn't really marry.'

'To be spared having to go home and eat sauerkraut?' she shot back.

'No, because they need to be familiar with all walks of life, to have a knowledge of casinos, say, international banks, Lebanese Maronites and Muslims, foreign restaurants in the Latin Quarter and Saint-Germain, Colombia's younger generation. Not to mention the Dutch language and beauty contests . . .'

'Are you finding a way through, though?'

She smiled, because he was gradually looking less worried.

'The next stage of the investigation will tell.'

He felt heavy when he got up, but only because he had done the food and beer too much justice. What a pleasure it would have been, after an almost sleepless night, to lie down on the bed and take a little siesta, vaguely aware of Madame Maigret moving around in the apartment!

'Are you off already?'

'Keulemans is meant to be calling me back from Amsterdam.'

She knew him too, because he had come to dinner more than once. Maigret called a taxi this time and waited for it outside as always. When he got to the office, he found Janvier was back.

'Any calls for me?'

'Only Lapointe. As there was almost nothing to eat in the refrigerator, Nahour's brother asked if he could get lunch delivered from a local delicatessen. Lapointe saw no reason to object, and in return they invited him to share their lunch. The two local inspectors have gone back to the station. The policeman on duty at the door has been relieved . . . Oh, I almost forgot: the young maid wouldn't touch the food. She made a big bowl of hot chocolate and dipped slices of bread into it.'

'Did Nahour and Ouéni eat at the same table?'

'Lapointe didn't say.'

'I want you to go to Boulevard Saint-Michel, where

you'll find a bar, the Bar des Tilleuls. It has a gaming room disguised as a private club on the first floor. The club's closed at the moment, but the entrance is in the bar.

'Tell the bar owner that Lardois sent you, and that we don't want to make any trouble for him. Try and find out if Fouad Ouéni went to the club last night and, if he did, what time he got there and what time he left.

'On your way back, drop in at a restaurant called the Petit Beyrouth on Rue des Bernardins. The owner is someone called Boutros. Félix Nahour was one of his real regulars. Did he have dinner yesterday in that restaurant? Was he alone? How long had he been going there without his wife? Was there a time when the couple were inseparable? That sort of thing. See what you can get out of him.'

Maigret hadn't touched the morning post, which was stacked in a pile on his blotter, next to the pipes. He reached a hand out for a letter, yawned, then decided to do it later. Siding down a little in his chair, he lowered his head and closed his eyes.

When the telephone startled him awake, no one was shaking him by the shoulder, there was no need to struggle. The clock said 3.30.

'Detective Chief Inspector Maigret? Hello, is that Detective Chief Inspector Maigret in person?'

The switchboard operator had a thick accent.

'This is Amsterdam. Stay on the line . . . I'm putting you through to Detective Chief Inspector Keulemans.'

Two or three clicks, then he heard the tall Dutch policeman's unfailingly cheery tones.

'Maigret? Keulemans here. Try and make a habit of giving me such easy jobs, will you? Naturally I found the landing cards at the airport. I didn't even have to leave the office; I had the contents read out to me over the telephone. The woman is, as you said, Evelina Nahour, née Wiemers, living in Paris, Avenue du Parc-Montsouris. She's younger than you thought. Twenty-seven. She was born in Amsterdam, that's true, but she left the city at a very young age with her parents when her father was made assistant manager of a dairy in Leeuwarden in Friesland.'

'Have you talked to her?'

'She's staying with her friend, Anna Keegel. The two women lived together for a few years when Lina was seventeen and her parents allowed her to come and work in Amsterdam.

'She started off as a switchboard operator at a travel agency, then graduated to receptionist for a well-known doctor and finally became a model for a couture house. Anna Keegel has always had the same job: a punch-card operator in a large brewery – I pointed out its warehouses when we went on a boat ride on the Amstel.'

'How did Lina Nahour react when you told her her husband was dead?'

'First of all, I should say that she was in bed and that her doctor had just left.'

'Did she tell you about her injury?'

'No. She said she was very tired.'

'Any sign of her friend?'

'The apartment consists of a large bedroom, a kitchen

and a bathroom, so I would have seen him if he'd been there. After a silence, she asked:

' "What did he die of?"

'I told her that I didn't know, but that she was needed for the reading of the will.'

'What did she say?'

'That she hoped to be well enough to fly tomorrow morning, although the doctor had prescribed plenty of rest. Just to be on the safe side I left one of my men in the neighbourhood. Unofficially, don't worry!'

'What about the Colombian?'

'Vicente Alvaredo, twenty-six, born in Bogotá, student, lives in Paris, Rue Notre-Dame-des-Champs.'

'Did you find him?'

'Easily. Also very unofficially, as I had the Lomanstraat apartment's telephone tapped. Lina Nahour picked it up before I'd left the street. She asked for the Rembrandt Hotel and was put through to Alvaredo. I've got the transcript of their conversation in front of me. Shall I read it out?'

Maigret's only regret was that he couldn't hold the receiver and fill a pipe at the same time. He looked longingly at the pipes lying in a neat, tempting row on his desk.

'It begins:

' "Vicente?"

' "Yes. Has the doctor been?"

' "Half an hour ago. He believed what I told him and he gave me some stitches after cleaning the wound. He's meant to be coming back tomorrow morning. I had another visit, someone from the police, a very tall, very nice man who told me my husband was dead . . ." '

A silence.

'You'll notice, Maigret, that the young man didn't ask any questions at that point.

' "The lawyer needs me for the reading of the will. I promised to get a plane tomorrow morning."

' "Do you think you'll be able to?"

' "My temperature's only thirty-eight. The doctor gave me some tablets, I don't know what sort, and now it hardly hurts at all."

' "Can I come and see you this afternoon?"

' "Not too early, because I'd like to get some sleep. My friend rang her office and told them she had flu. Apparently a third of the staff are in bed. She's taking good care of me."

' "I'll be there around five." '

Another silence.

'That's it, Maigret. They started talking in English and carried on in French. Anything else I can do?'

'I'd like to know if she gets the flight and, if so, what time she'll be at Orly. Naturally I'd also like an update on Alvaredo . . .'

'Unofficially!' Keulemans laughed, then signed off like Maigret's colleagues with a cheery 'Bye, chief!'

4.

It was a slow afternoon in the stuffy office, and the six or seven pipes lined up on his desk had all been smoked. Almost every investigation had what Maigret called the gap, a moment when a certain amount of information had been gathered but not yet checked, so couldn't be used.

It was a quiet but frustrating time because the temptation was to construct theories, to draw conclusions that might easily be wrong.

If Maigret had followed his inclination, rather than tell himself that a detective chief inspector's job was not to run around everywhere like a hunting dog, he would have seen everything for himself, as he used to when he was still just an inspector.

For instance, he envied Keulemans seeing Lina Nahour and her unprepossessing friend in the Amsterdam apartment which the two young women used to share.

He would also have liked to have taken Lapointe's place and spent the whole day in the house on Avenue du Parc-Montsouris, nosing around, sniffing in corners, opening drawers at random, studying Fouad Ouéni, Pierre Nahour and the disconcerting Nelly, who was perhaps not as infantile as she was trying to make believe.

He wasn't following any preconceived plan. He was

going forwards, wherever that might be, trying above all not to form any opinions.

He smiled when there was a knock at the door and he saw the Pardons' maid come into his office.

'Hello, Monsieur Maigret.'

As far as she was concerned he was the monthly dinner guest, not a detective chief inspector with the Police Judiciaire.

'I'm bringing you the report. Monsieur told me to make sure I gave it to you personally.'

It had been typed with two fingers on the doctor's old typewriter, and was studded with crossings-out, missing letters and words run together.

Had Pardon started writing it the night before, after Maigret had left? Or had he written it a few lines at a time between patients? Maigret glanced through it, breaking into a smile as he saw how meticulous his friend had been, the effort he had visibly taken not to omit any detail as if he were giving a medical diagnosis.

He had no time to sit around pondering, though, because he was told there were journalists waiting for him in the corridor. He hesitated, then ended up muttering:

'Send them in.'

There were five of them, plus a couple of photographers, and one of the reporters was young Maquille, who, despite being just twenty and cherubic-looking, was one of the most dogged members of the Parisian press.

'What can you tell us about the Nahour case?'

Ah! It was already the Nahour case – no doubt that is what all the papers would call it.

'Not much, boys. It's early days.'

'Do you think Nahour could have committed suicide?'

'Definitely not. We have proof he didn't because the bullet that lodged in his skull after passing through his throat is of a different calibre to the gun found under his body.'

'He was holding the gun in his hand when he was killed, was he?'

'Probably. As I can foresee what you're going to ask next, I'll tell you straight away that I don't know who was in the room at the time.'

'What about in the house?' inquired young Maquille.

'A young Dutch maid, Nelly Velthuis, was asleep on the first floor, in a room at some distance from the studio. Apparently she's a heavy sleeper and says she didn't hear anything.'

'Wasn't there a secretary too?'

They must have questioned the neighbours, perhaps even the local shopkeepers.

'Until proven otherwise, the secretary, Fouad Ouéni, was in town and didn't return until one thirty in the morning. He couldn't get into the studio and went straight up to bed.'

'Madame Nahour?'

'She was away.'

'Before or after the tragedy?' the persistent Maquille went on, choosing his words carefully.

'The question remains unresolved.'

'But there's still a question?'

'There are always questions.'

'That it might be a political crime, for instance?'

'Félix Nahour wasn't involved in politics, as far as we know.'

'What about his brother in Geneva?'

They had made more headway than Maigret expected.

'Wasn't his bank a cover for other activities?'

'You're going too fast for me.'

All the same, Maigret resolved to check that Pierre Nahour had definitely arrived in Paris on the morning flight. So far there was no proof he hadn't been in town the day before.

'Had the gun found under the victim's body been fired?'

'It's with the experts and I haven't got their report yet,' Maigret answered noncommittally. 'Right, you know pretty much as much as I do now, and I'll ask you to let me get on with my work. I'll be sure to call you in when I have any news.'

He knew for a fact that Maquille was going to leave one of his colleagues in the corridor to watch his office and make a note of any visitors.

'Is . . . ?'

'No, boys! I've got a lot to do, that's all the time I can give you.'

It hadn't gone too badly. He sighed, imagining a nicely chilled glass of beer, but couldn't quite bring himself to get one sent up from the Brasserie Dauphine.

'Hello? Lapointe? What's happening over there?'

'The house is as gloomy as ever. The cleaner is furious we're not letting her do any housework. Nelly is lying on her bed, reading an English crime novel. And Pierre Nahour is shut away in the office, going through all the correspondence and papers in the drawers.'

'Has he made any telephone calls?'

'Only one, to Beirut, to tell his father. The old man is trying to get a seat on the next plane.'

'Put Pierre Nahour on, will you?'

'He's right here.'

The next thing he heard was the voice of the banker from Geneva.

'Yes . . .'

'Do you know if your brother had a lawyer in Paris?'

'Félix mentioned him last time we saw each other, three years ago. He said that if he died his will would be in the possession of Maître Leroy-Beaudieu on Boulevard Saint-Germain. I happen to know Leroy-Beaudieu very well because I did some of my law studies with him, although we haven't been in touch much since then.'

'Did your brother tell you what was in his will?'

'No. He only said rather resentfully that despite our father's criticisms he was still a Nahour.'

'Have you found anything in the papers you're going through?'

'Bills, mostly, which suggest my sister-in-law didn't deal with the tradesmen, even the butcher and greengrocer, choosing to leave that chore to my brother. Almost daily reports from the nanny with news of the children, which show my brother was very attached to them. Invitations, letters from casino managers and croupiers.'

'Look, Monsieur Nahour. You don't have to stay in the house any more. You can go anywhere in Paris, as long as you don't leave the city. If you take a hotel room . . .'

'I have no intention of doing that. I'll sleep in my brother's room. I may go out, if only for dinner.'

'Will you pass me back to my inspector? Hello, Lapointe? I've just given Pierre Nahour permission to come and go as he sees fit. The same does not apply to Ouéni, and I'd rather the maid didn't leave the house either.

'The cleaner can do her shopping and then go home if she wants.

'I'll send someone to relieve you towards the end of the afternoon. Goodbye for now.'

He went into the inspectors' office, where fifteen or so inspectors were working, some typing up reports, others making telephone calls.

'Who here speaks English more or less fluently?'

They looked at each other in silence until Baron shyly raised his hand.

'I should warn you that I've got a terrible accent.'

'You're going to take over from Lapointe at Avenue du Parc-Montsouris between five and six and spend the night there. He'll tell you more.'

When he returned to his office soon afterwards, Maigret found Janvier in his overcoat; he had brought a blast of freezing air in from outside.

'I've seen the owner of the Bar des Tilleuls, a fat, sleepy character who I suspect is far smarter than he'd like people to think. He claims that his only connection with the club upstairs, which is run by someone called Pozzi, is that punters have to go through his place to get there.

'The bar's full between eight and eleven, or midnight, because lots of people come to watch television.

'It was even fuller than usual yesterday because the

wrestling was on. He didn't see Ouéni come in but he saw him leave around a quarter past one.'

'So Ouéni could have got there any time before a quarter past one and only stayed a few minutes in the club?'

'It's possible. If you want, I'll go and question Pozzi and the croupiers tonight, and, if necessary, the regulars.'

Maigret would have liked to go too. He hesitated before admitting that he'd be better off getting some rest after his almost sleepless night. Tomorrow promised to be busy.

'What about the restaurant?'

'It's tiny, with such a strong smell of Middle Eastern cooking it made my head spin. Boutros is a portly character who splays his feet out as he waddles along. Apparently he had no idea what happened last night because when I told him Nahour was dead he started crying.

' "My best customer! My brother!" he exclaimed. "Yes, that's right, inspector, I loved that man like a brother. He used to come and eat here when he was a student, and I often gave him credit for weeks. When he became rich, though, he didn't forget poor old Boutros and if he was in Paris he'd come and eat here almost every evening.

' "Look! There's his table, in the corner, by the bar." '

'Did he talk to you about Madame Nahour?'

'He's one of those old devils who watch you out of the corner of their eye as they he put on a great show. He went into raptures for hours about Madame Nahour's beauty, her sweetness, her kindness.

' "And she's not a bit stuck-up, inspector! She always shakes my hand when she arrives and when she leaves." '

'When did he see her last?'

'He doesn't know. He's very vague. In the early days of their marriage she used to come in with her husband more often than she had done recently, that was true. They were an attractive couple, very much in love. They had always been very in love. No, nothing went wrong between them, but of course she had to look after the house and the children.'

'Doesn't he know the children live on the Riviera?'

'He pretends not to, at any rate.'

Maigret couldn't help smiling. Everyone was lying in this case, weren't they? It had started at Pardon's the night before with that unbelievable story of the shot from a car and the old woman pointing out the doctor's building.

'Wait a second,' Maigret told Janvier, 'I need to make a call. Stay here.'

He got Lapointe on the telephone again.

'Has the cleaner left?'

'I think I can hear her getting ready to go.'

'Put her on, will you?'

He had to wait a while before a woman's voice asked bluntly:

'What do you want now?'

'To ask you a question, Madame Bodin. How long have you lived in the fourteenth arrondissement?'

'I don't know what that's got to do with . . .'

'I can easily ask at the station, where I'm sure you're registered.'

'Three years.'

'And where did you live before?'

'Rue Servan, in the eleventh.'

'Were you ill there?'

'My health is no one's business.'

'But you went to Doctor Pardon, didn't you?'

'He's a good man, that doctor – never asks people questions, just makes them better.'

So a little mystery that had been bothering Maigret since he had heard Pardon's story had been resolved.

'Is that all? Can I go and do my shopping?'

'One more thing. You were fond of Doctor Pardon, so you probably sent people you knew to him, did you?'

'I might have.'

'Try to remember. Who did you mention him to in the house you're working in now?'

There was a fairly long silence, during which Maigret could hear the old woman breathing.

'I've no idea.'

'Madame Nahour?'

'She's never been ill.'

'Monsieur Ouéni? The maid?'

'I'm telling you, I don't even remember mentioning him to anyone! Honestly, if I can't even go and do my shopping, you might as well arrest me.'

Maigret hung up. His pipe had gone out, and he asked Janvier to ring Orly as he filled another.

'Ask the inspector if the flight that landed just after eleven was Air-France or Swissair.'

Janvier repeated the question to the person on the other end of the line.

'Swissair?' Janvier said. 'Wait a second . . .'

'Get him to put you through to the office that registers arrivals.'

'Hello! Can you . . .'

A few minutes later Maigret had cleared up something else. Pierre Nahour had definitely arrived that morning from Geneva on a Metropolitan in which he had got a seat at the last minute.

'What now, chief?'

'As you see, I'm checking. Do you know what time Félix Nahour had dinner yesterday evening?'

'Around eight thirty. He left just after nine thirty. He had lamb and an almond and raisin cake.'

'Go next door and pass that on to Doctor Colinet, who needs it to establish the time of death.'

Then Maigret looked up Maître Leroy-Beaudieu's telephone number, thinking the name was familiar. When he got him on the telephone, the lawyer exclaimed:

'What news, my dear detective chief inspector? It's a very long time since I had the pleasure of seeing or hearing you.'

As Maigret racked his brains, the lawyer went on:

'The Montrond case, do you remember? That old client of mine whose wife . . .'

'Yes . . . Yes.'

'What can I do for you?'

'I believe the will of someone called Félix Nahour is in your possession.'

'Very true . . . He cancelled the old one and wrote a new one about two years ago.'

'Do you know why he changed his mind?'

83

There was an embarrassed silence.

'It's a delicate matter, and I am in an awkward position . . . Monsieur Nahour has never confided in me and, as far as the will itself is concerned, as you will realize I am bound by professional confidentiality. But, if it's of any help, I can tell you that the reasons were purely personal.'

'Félix Nahour was murdered last night in his office.'

'Oh! There hasn't been anything in the newspapers.'

'There will be in the next editions.'

'Has the murderer been arrested?'

'We've only been able to make contradictory assumptions so far. Isn't it quite common – I think you will be able to tell me this – when a husband writes his will that the wife writes hers at the same time?'

'I've known that to happen.'

'With Monsieur and Madame Nahour?'

'I've never met Madame Nahour and I've never had any dealings with her. She's a former beauty queen, isn't she?'

'That's right.'

'When is the funeral?'

'I don't know because the body is still with the pathologist.'

'We normally wait for the funeral before we get in touch with the people concerned. Do you think it will take a while?'

'It might.'

'Have you informed the family?'

'His brother, Pierre Nahour, arrived in Paris this morning. His father, who was still in Beirut at midday, has apparently taken the first plane.'

'What about Madame Nahour?'

'We're expecting her tomorrow morning.'

'Listen, my dear detective chief inspector, I'll send out the notifications this evening. Would you like the will to be read the day after tomorrow, in the afternoon?'

'That would suit me.'

'I'd like to help as much as I can, without infringing our professional rules. All I can tell you is that Madame Nahour, if she was aware of the first will, is going to have quite an unpleasant surprise when she reads the second. Is that useful?'

'Very. Thank you, maître.'

Janvier had come back into Maigret's office.

'There's been a development,' Maigret muttered wryly. 'If I've understood correctly, Madame Nahour was the principal beneficiary of the first will. Around two years ago, the husband wrote a second one, and I'd be surprised if he's left his wife more than the legal minimum.'

'You think that she . . .'

'You're forgetting that I don't think anything until the end of an investigation.'

He added with a sceptical smile:

'If then.'

It was definitely an afternoon for telephone calls.

'Get me the Pension des Palmiers in Mougins.'

He rummaged in his pockets and fished out a scrap of paper on which he had written the nanny's name.

'See if Mademoiselle Jobé is there.'

He went and stood by the window because he felt numb from sitting in his chair so long. The snowflakes were thinning. The streetlights had been on for a while – in some places all day.

A traffic jam had brought Pont Saint-Michel to a halt. Three uniformed policemen were trying to disentangle the snarl of cars and buses, blowing loudly on their whistles.

'Hello? That's Mademoiselle Jobé, is it? One moment, please, I'll put Detective Chief Inspector Maigret on . . . No . . . Police Judiciaire, in Paris.'

Maigret took the call standing up, a thigh propped on his desk.

'Hello, Mademoiselle Jobé? The two children are with you, I imagine . . . What? You haven't been able to go out because of the rain and the cold. Well, if it's any comfort, the snow's making driving almost impossible here in Paris . . .

'I'm wondering if you've heard from Monsieur Nahour . . . He rang you yesterday? Roughly at what time? Ten in the morning . . . Yes, I understand. He either rings before their walk or in the evening. Did he have a special reason for calling? Nothing particular . . . He does so two or three times a week.

'What about Madame Nahour? Not so often, once a week . . . Sometimes she doesn't call for a fortnight . . .

'No, mademoiselle, I'm asking you these questions because Monsieur Nahour was murdered last night . . . No one has been arrested . . . May I ask how long you've been working for the family? Five years. So, since the birth of the first child . . .

'Unfortunately I can't come to Mougins at the

moment . . . I may have to authorize Cannes' Crime Squad to take your statement . . . Oh no! Don't worry at all. I understand your situation.

'Listen, when you started working, the Nahours travelled a lot, didn't they? Yes . . . Cannes sometimes, Deauville, Evian . . . Most of the time they rented a villa for the season or some of it. Did you go with them? You often did. Yes, I can hear you perfectly.

'You lived in the Ritz with them and the little girl. Then, three years later, the boy was born, is that it? He's not a sickly child who needs a warmer climate than Paris, is he? . . . He's two now, if I'm not mistaken . . . And a rascal, I see . . .

'Of course . . . Off you go . . . I'll stay on the line.'

He told Janvier:

'The kids are fighting in the next room. She seems a lovely girl. She answers clearly, no hesitation – long may it last!

'Hello? Yes . . . So, Monsieur Nahour was more involved with the children than his wife . . . You sent him a short report every day on their health and what they were doing.

'Did you notice any tension between the husband and wife? Hard to tell, I know . . . They each had their own life . . . That didn't surprise you? Only at first? You got used to it . . .

'Did they come to see them together? Hardly ever? I am very grateful for your help . . . You don't know any more than that, I quite understand . . . Thank you, mademoiselle . . .'

Maigret sighed deeply and relit his pipe, which he had let go out.

'And now for the tedious part . . . Actually I only say that out of habit because Examining Magistrate Cayotte is a good sort.'

He picked up Doctor Pardon's report from his desk and leisurely made his way to the examining magistrates' corner of the Palais de Justice. Cayotte hadn't been eligible for modern offices, and his room was straight out of a nineteenth-century novel.

Even the clerk seemed out of a drawing by Forain or Steinlen and could easily have been wearing oversleeves.

Files were piled up on the floor for lack of space on the black wooden shelves, and the light over the magistrate's desk had lost its shade.

'Sit down, Maigret . . . Well?'

Maigret didn't conceal anything. For over an hour he sat on an uncomfortable chair spelling out everything he knew. When he finally left, the smoke from his pipe and the chain-smoking magistrate's cigarettes hung in a thick pall around the lightbulb.

Maigret was at the airport by 9.30 a.m., even though the flight from Amsterdam wasn't expected until 9.57. It was Sunday. As he was shaving he had heard the radio advising people not to drive unless absolutely necessary because the snow crust on the roads had become harder and more slippery than ever.

Lucas had driven him and was waiting outside in the Police Judiciaire car. The airport concourse was busier than Paris's streets, and the air in there was warm, almost body temperature, making the blood rush to his head.

After having a glass of beer at one of the bars, Maigret felt scarlet in the face and regretted loading himself down with the stifling scarf Madame Maigret had knitted and insisted he wear.

The loudspeakers announced that the Copenhagen flight via Amsterdam was going to be delayed by around ten minutes. He paced up and down, looking at the policemen who were checking passports at Arrivals, glancing briefly at the travellers' faces and stamping or not stamping their passports accordingly.

The day before, at around eight in the evening, Keulemans had telephoned him at Boulevard Richard-Lenoir just as he was sitting down to watch television.

'Lina Nahour has booked two seats on the 8.45 flight to Orly.'

'Is Alvaredo going with her?'

'No. The second seat is for her friend Anna Keegel. The young man booked a seat on the 11.22 flight, which gets into Paris at twelve forty-five.'

'Have they talked on the telephone again?'

'This afternoon, about five. Lina Nahour gave him the time of her flight, adding that her friend was going with her. He said he would get the next flight. When he asked how she was, she said she felt very well and that her temperature was down to 37.5.'

The flight's arrival was finally announced. Maigret went and pressed his face against the cold window, his eyes following the customary bustle of activity around the plane.

He couldn't recognize the woman he was looking for among the first batch of passengers, which included four children, and was starting to worry she had changed her mind when he saw a young woman dressed in a sealskin coat leaning on her friend's arm as she came down the stairs.

Anna Keegel, a short brunette, was wearing a bulky woollen coat in a distinctive shade of acid green.

At the last moment, the air hostess helped Lina into the little shuttle bus, which was already crammed with the other passengers, and the door shut immediately behind them.

Having been last off the aeroplane, the two women were also last to show their passports, and Maigret, leaning against the window, had time to study them closely.

Was Lina Nahour really beautiful? It was a matter of taste. She had the fair, almost golden Nordic complexion Pardon had mentioned, with a little pointed nose and porcelain-blue eyes.

Her features were drawn that morning, and it was clearly a huge effort for her to stand upright.

Anna Keegel, on the other hand, was ugly yet appealing and, although there was nothing humorous about the situation, looked as if she was quick to laugh.

Keeping a discreet distance, Maigret followed them to customs, where they waited a few minutes for a green suitcase and another, cheaper-looking bag which must have belonged to Anna.

A porter took their luggage and hailed a taxi for them outside. Maigret got back into the police car next to Lucas.

'Is that them?'

'Yes. Don't let them give you the slip.'

It wasn't hard to keep up with them, because the taxi-driver drove carefully, and they took three-quarters of an hour to reach Parc Montsouris.

'Did you think they'd go somewhere else?'

'I didn't think anything. I just wanted to make sure. Stop behind the taxi when it parks and wait for me.'

The two women got out. Lina Nahour looked the house up and down, as if she were hesitating, before finally letting her friend help her through the garden gate.

Maigret overtook them and reached the foot of the steps before they did.

'Who are you?' Lina asked, frowning.

She had a very slight accent.

'Detective Chief Inspector Maigret. I am investigating your husband's death. May I follow you in . . . ?'

She didn't object but seemed more on edge, hugging her coat more tightly to her. The driver brought the luggage, which he left on the steps, and Anna Keegel opened her handbag to pay the fare.

The bulky figure of Torrence, who had taken the day shift, opened the door without a word. Lina looked at him with surprise more than concern.

It was obvious she didn't know what to do or where to go, whether to go up to her room or into the studio.

'Where's the body?' she asked Maigret.

'At the Forensic Institute.'

Was she relieved it wasn't in the house any more? She seemed to shudder but she was so tense that her movements were reflexes as much as anything.

Finally she put her hand on the studio's door handle, and as she was about to turn it, the door was opened from inside and Pierre Nahour appeared, surprised to find four people in the corridor.

'Hello, Pierre,' she said, holding out her hand.

Did the Geneva banker really hesitate? Either way he held out his hand too.

'Where did it happen?'

Pierre Nahour stepped back to let Lina, her friend and Maigret go in, while Torrence remained in the corridor.

'Here . . . Behind the desk.'

She took a few tentative steps, saw the bloodstain and looked away.

'How did they do it?'

'They shot him.'

'Did he die straight away?'

Pierre Nahour remained calm, cool even, observing his sister-in-law without any obvious emotion on his face.

'We don't know. The cleaner found him when she started work yesterday morning.'

Sensing that she was unsteady on her feet, Lina's friend led her to a chair, where she sat down gingerly, presumably because her back was hurting. She motioned that she wanted a cigarette, and Anna Keegel lit one and passed it to her.

There was a pained silence. Maigret felt concerned about the young woman's physical and, most likely, emotional state; her nerves must have been stretched to breaking point.

'We don't know if he suffered, do we?'

'We don't,' Pierre Nahour said curtly.

'What time did it . . . did it happen?'

'Probably between midnight and one in the morning.'

'Wasn't there anyone in the house?'

'Fouad was at the club, and Nelly was sleeping. She says she didn't hear anything.'

'Is it true that I have to go to a meeting at the lawyer's?'

'He rang me, yes. Tomorrow afternoon. My father arrived last night and he's resting at the Hôtel Raspail.'

'What am I going to do?' she asked no one in particular.

After an even more unpleasant silence, her friend said something to her in Dutch.

'Do you think?' Lina asked in French. 'Yes. That might be better. I wouldn't be up to sleeping in this house.'

She looked around for Maigret.

'I'm going to stay in a hotel with my friend and my maid.'

She wasn't asking permission, like a suspect, just reporting what she had decided.

Then she turned back to her brother-in-law:

'Is Nelly upstairs? Where's Madame Bodin?'

'She didn't come today. Nelly is in her room.'

'I'm going up to get some underwear and a change of clothes. Will you come and help, Anna?'

Left alone, the two men looked at one another in silence.

'How did your father take it, Monsieur Nahour?'

'Pretty badly. My sister came with him, and they've both gone to the hotel to have a rest. I insisted they shouldn't stay here.'

'Are you going to?'

'I'd rather. Are you forming a sense of the murderer's personality, Monsieur Maigret?'

'Are you?'

'I don't know. Why didn't you question my sister-in-law?'

'I'm waiting for her to be settled in the hotel. She probably can't take any more at the moment.'

Both of them were standing, and Pierre Nahour had a hard look on his face.

'I'd like to ask you a question,' Maigret said slowly. 'You've read your brother's correspondence and had a chance to talk to Ouéni. He doesn't seem prepared to cooperate with us. Perhaps, with you . . .'

'I tried to get something out of him last night, without much success.'

'The number of possible suspects seems relatively limited, on one condition . . .'

'What?'

'Suppose that, contrary to your first assumption, your brother wasn't just gambling for himself recently, that he was working for a syndicate, as he had done in the past.'

'I see what you're getting at but please, detective chief inspector, don't waste your time on such theories. My brother was an honest man, like all the Nahours. He was scrupulous to the point of persnicketiness, in fact, as I've realized going through his correspondence.

'The notion of him cheating a syndicate out of any money – even out of a centime – and then being killed in revenge is unthinkable.'

'I'm glad to hear you say that. I'm sorry my job means

I have to entertain every hypothesis. Maybe it was Ouéni's presence in the house that gave me the idea.'

'I don't understand.'

'Doesn't Ouéni's situation seem suspect to you? He's not a secretary exactly, or a valet or driver, but nor is he an equal. So it's not that far-fetched to think that he could have been the syndicate's representative, keeping tabs on your brother.'

Nahour gave an ironic smile.

'If anyone else said that to me I'd tell him he'd been reading too many crime novels. I told you how seriously the Lebanese take family. Well, family for them isn't just relatives, close or otherwise. Old retainers can be part of the family, friends who live in the house on an equal footing . . .'

'Would you have chosen Ouéni?'

'No. For one thing because I don't like the man, for another because I married young, and my wife is enough for me. Don't forget that Félix remained a bachelor until he was thirty-five. The family was convinced he would never get married.'

'If you'll excuse me . . .'

Hearing footsteps on the stairs, Maigret went to open the door. Lina had changed her dress and was wearing her mink coat now. Nelly Velthuis followed behind, a faraway look in her eyes, carrying a suitcase, and Anna Keegel brought up the rear with more bags.

'Do you mind calling me a taxi, Pierre? I shouldn't have sent mine away.'

She gave Maigret a questioning look, and he asked:

'Which hotel are you going to? The Ritz?'

'Oh no, that would bring back too many memories. Wait, what's that hotel on the corner of Rue de Rivoli called, near Place de la Vendôme?'

'The Hôtel du Louvre?'

'That's it. We're going to the Hôtel du Louvre.'

'I'll call in there soon, if I may, because I have to ask you some questions.'

'The taxi's on its way.'

It was almost midday. Janvier would be arriving at Orly, where he was going to wait for Alvaredo and then tail him.

'Goodbye, Pierre. What time is the meeting tomorrow, and what lawyer's is it at?'

'Three, at Maître Leroy-Beaudieu's on Boulevard Saint-Germain.'

'You don't need to write it down,' Maigret put in. 'I'll give you the address at the hotel.'

It took a while to fit the luggage and the three passengers into the car. Lina was shaking visibly as she stood on the pavement, looking around as if she didn't recognize the familiar surroundings.

Pierre Nahour had shut the door of the house, and Maigret thought a curtain was moving in what must have been Ouéni's window.

Taking his seat next to Lucas, he said:

'Follow them. They're going to the Hôtel du Louvre, but I'd like to be sure. I'm not convinced I've heard anyone say a word of truth in this business so far.'

The streets were as deserted as in August, without the coaches full of tourists. The taxi stopped outside the Hôtel du Louvre. Lina and her friend went in first, doubtless to check whether they had rooms free. A few moments later a porter came out to get the luggage while the maid looked at the meter and paid the fare.

'Go and park the car somewhere and meet me in the bar. I've got to allow her time to get to her room and make herself comfortable.'

Besides, he was thirsty.

5.

The bar was dark and silent. Two Englishmen sitting on high stools were moving their lips, but he couldn't hear what they were saying. The walls were oak-panelled, and the bronze wall lamps at intervals of four or five metres only shed a discreet light. A young woman was waiting in a corner, a reddish cocktail on the table in front of her. Four men in the opposite corner bent towards each other from time to time.

It was Sunday here too, a slack day removed from reality. Through the cream curtains he could just see a little dirty snow, some black trees, a head as someone walked past.

'Cloakroom, sir?'

'I'm sorry . . .'

His investigations more often took him to local cafés or noisy bars around the Champs-Élysées than luxury hotels. He took off his overcoat and gave a sigh of relief as he unwound his stifling scarf.

'A beer,' he ordered in a low voice from the barman, who was staring at him as if trying to remember where he had seen his face.

'Carlsberg, Heineken?'

'Any will do.'

The trusty Lucas was also stopped by the coat-check girl.

'What are you having?'

'What about you, chief?'

'I ordered a beer.'

'The same, then.'

The words 'Grill Room' were spelled out in discreet neon above an open door, through which came the quiet chink of plates.

'Are you hungry?'

'Not very.'

'Do you know their room numbers?'

'437, 438 and 439. Two bedrooms and a small sitting room.'

'What about Nelly?'

'She's sleeping in one of the bedrooms. The other one, 437, is a big room with twin beds for Madame Nahour and her friend.'

'I'll be right back.'

Out in the huge marble corridor, Maigret headed towards a door marked 'Telephone'.

'Can you put me through to 437, please?'

'One moment . . .'

'Hello? Madame Nahour?'

'Who's calling?'

'Detective Chief Inspector Maigret.'

'This is Anna Keegel. Madame Nahour is in the bath.'

'Ask her if she'd rather I came up in a quarter of an hour or after she has had lunch.'

He waited, hearing only a confused murmur of voices.

'Hello? She's not hungry because she ate on the plane, but she'd rather you left it for half an hour before coming up.'

A few minutes later Maigret and Lucas went into the grill, which was as hushed as the bar, with the same oak panelling and wall lights and little lamps on the tables. Only three or four tables were occupied, and everyone was whispering as if they were in church. The maître d'hôtel, headwaiters and waiters padded about in silence like officiants at a service.

Maigret shook his head as he was presented with a huge menu.

'Cold cuts,' he muttered.

'Me too.'

'Two charcuterie plates,' the maître d'hôtel said, correcting them.

'And some beer.'

'I'll send the wine waiter over.'

'Will you ring headquarters to tell them we're here? Someone needs to get word to Janvier, who'll still be at Orly. Give him the number of the apartment.'

Maigret felt heavy suddenly, and Lucas, recognizing the signs, took care not to ask him superfluous questions.

They ate in virtual silence, watched by the maître d'hôtel and some waiters.

'Will you be having coffee?'

A man in Turkish national dress served it with a great rigmarole.

'You'd better come up with me.'

They took the lift to the fourth floor, found room 437 and knocked on the door, but it was the door to room 438 that opened.

'This way,' Anna Keegel said.

She must have had a bath or a shower too, because her hair was still slightly wet.

'Come in. I'll go and tell Lina.'

In the sitting room, which wasn't large, everything was soft and smooth: pale-grey walls, chairs of an equally delicate blue, a table painted ivory. Someone could be heard moving around in the room on the left, probably Nelly Velthuis still unpacking.

They waited for quite a long time, awkwardly standing around, until finally the two women came in. Maigret was surprised because he had been expecting to find Lina Nahour in bed.

She had just done her hair and wasn't wearing any make-up. She had put on a dusty-pink velours dressing gown.

She seemed frail, vulnerable. If it was an effort for her to see them, though, it didn't show, and the morning's tension had disappeared.

She was surprised to see two men rather than Maigret on his own, as she'd been expecting. She stood looking at Lucas for a moment, as if uncertain what to do.

'One of my inspectors,' explained Maigret.

'Have a seat, gentlemen.'

She sat on the sofa herself, and her friend came and sat beside her.

'I'm sorry to disturb you when you've only just got here but as I'm sure you'll understand, madame, I have a few questions to ask you.'

She lit a cigarette, and the fingers holding the match trembled a little.

'You can smoke,' she said.

'Thank you.'

He didn't fill his pipe immediately.

'May I ask where you were on Friday night?'

'What time?'

'I'd rather you told me your movements that night.'

'I left the house around eight in the evening.'

'Roughly at the same time as your husband, then.'

'I don't know where he was at that point.'

'Were you in the habit of going out like that without telling him where you were going?'

'We were both free to come and go as we pleased.'

'Did you take your car?'

'No. The roads were icy, and I didn't want to drive.'

'Did you call a taxi?'

'Yes.'

'From the telephone in your bedroom?'

'Yes. Of course.'

She talked in the voice of a little girl reciting her homework, and her innocent eyes reminded Maigret of something. It was only after she had answered a few questions that he thought of the maid, her almost transparent pupils, her childlike expressions.

He recognized the same mannerisms in Lina, the same expressions, even down to a way of hurriedly batting her eyelids, which suggested one of the two women had copied the other.

'Where did it take you?'

'To a big restaurant on the Champs-Élysées, the Marignan.'

She hesitated before saying the last word.

'Did you often eat at the Marignan?'

'Sometimes.'

'On your own?'

'Mostly.'

'Where were you sitting?'

'In the main room.'

Which seated a hundred-odd customers, so her alibi couldn't be checked.

'Did anyone join you?'

'No.'

'You hadn't arranged to meet anyone?'

'I was on my own the whole time.'

'Until when?'

'I don't know. Ten, maybe.'

'You didn't go to the bar first?'

Another hesitation before she shook her head.

Now the more nervous of the two of them was her friend, Anna Keegel, who looked back and forth from Lina to Maigret, turning her head each time they said something.

'And then?'

'I went for a little walk along the Champs-Élysées to get some air.'

'Even though the pavements were slippery?'

'The pavements had been cleared. I got a taxi by the Lido, and it took me home.'

'Again you didn't see your husband, even though he got back around ten?'

'I didn't see him. I went up to my room, where Nelly was finishing packing my suitcase.'

'Because you'd decided to go on a trip?'

'A week ago,' she replied with complete candour.

'Where to?'

'Um . . . Amsterdam of course.'

Then she said something to Anna Keegel in Dutch. Her friend stood up, went into the bedroom and promptly came back with a letter. Dated 6 January, it wasn't written in French or English.

'You can have that translated. I'm telling Anna I'll be arriving on 15 January.'

'Did you book your plane ticket?'

'No. I thought I'd take the train at first. There's one at eleven twelve.'

'Weren't you intending to take your maid?'

'There isn't any room for her in Anna's apartment.'

Even though he wanted to let her tie herself completely in knots, Maigret couldn't help feeling a sort of admiration for the quiet candour with which she reeled off her lies.

'Didn't you look in on the ground floor when you left?'

'No. The taxi Nelly had called was already at the kerb.'

'Didn't you say goodbye to your husband?'

'No. He knew what was happening.'

'Did you ask to be taken to the Gare du Nord?'

'We got there late because of the bad state of the roads. The train had left, so I got the taxi to drop me at Orly.'

'By way of Boulevard Voltaire?'

She didn't even start. Keegel blinked, however.

'Where's that?'

'I'm sorry to have to say that you know as well as I do. How did you get Doctor Pardon's address?'

There was a long silence. She lit another cigarette, got up and walked around the room, then came and sat back down. She wasn't obviously troubled. If anything, she seemed to be running through different possible ways to respond.

'What do you know?' she countered finally, looking Maigret in the eye.

'That you were wounded in the studio by a bullet fired by your husband from a pearl-handled 6.35 which used to belong to you and which he kept in a drawer of his desk.'

Propping her arm on the arm-rest, she cupped her chin in her hand and looked intently at Maigret with what appeared to be curiosity. She might have been a model pupil listening to her teacher.

'You didn't leave the house in a taxi but in a red car belonging to a friend of yours called Vicente Alvaredo. He drove you to Boulevard Voltaire, where he told a far-fetched story of you being attacked by a stranger in a car.

'You didn't say a word as Dr Pardon put a temporary dressing on the wound. Then you went back into his office and as he was taking off his coat and washing his hands, you slipped out.'

'What do you want from me?'

She was completely unruffled. She might almost have been smiling, again like a little girl who's been caught lying but doesn't think it's such a great sin.

'I want the truth.'

'I'd rather you asked me questions.'

That was clever too, because it meant she could find out exactly what the police knew. Maigret played along all the same.

'Was this letter really written on January the 6th? Before you answer, you should know that we can check by analysing the ink.'

'It was written on January the 6th.'

'Did your husband know?'

'He must have suspected.'

'Suspected what?'

'That I'd be leaving soon.'

'Why?'

'Because life hadn't been bearable for a long time.'

'How long?'

'Months.'

'Two years?'

'Maybe.'

'Since you met Vicente Alvaredo?'

Anna Keegel was becoming increasingly jumpy and, as if by accident, her foot nudged Lina's red slipper.

'That's right, more or less.'

'Did your husband know about your affair?'

'I don't know. Someone may have seen us, Vicente and me. We weren't hiding.'

'Do you think it normal for a married woman—'

'Hardly!'

'What do you mean?'

'Félix and I had been living as strangers for years.'

'And yet two years ago you had another child.'

'Because my husband was desperate to have a son. Luckily I didn't have another girl.'

'Is he the father of your son?'

'Definitely. I met Alvaredo after I had given birth, when I was just starting to go out.'

'Have you had other lovers?'

'You might find it hard to believe, but he was the first.'

'What had you planned for the evening of the 14th?'

'I don't understand.'

'On the 6th you wrote to your friend that you would be in Amsterdam on the 15th.'

Anna Keegel started talking to her in Dutch, but Lina shook her head firmly and carried on looking at Maigret in the same self-assured way.

Maigret had finally lit his pipe.

'I'll try to explain. Alvaredo wanted me to get a divorce so I could marry him. I asked him for a week because I knew it wouldn't be easy. There's never been a divorce in the Nahour family, and Félix wanted to keep up appearances.

'We decided that I would talk to him on the 14th and then, however he reacted, we'd go straight to Amsterdam.'

'Why Amsterdam?'

She seemed surprised that Maigret didn't understand.

'Because it's the city where I spent a lot of my childhood and my life when I was single. Vicente didn't know Holland. I wanted to show it to him. Once the divorce had gone through, we were going to see his parents in Colombia before we got married.'

'Are you wealthy in your own right?'

'No, of course not. But we don't need the Nahours' money.'

She added with a hint of naive pride:

'The Alvaredos are richer than them and they own most of Colombia's goldmines.'

'Right. So you left around eight without saying anything to your husband. Alvaredo was waiting for you in the Alfa Romeo. Where did you have dinner?'

'In a little restaurant on Boulevard Montparnasse where Vicente has almost all his meals because he lives round the corner.'

'Were you worried how your husband might react when he found out what you'd decided?'

'No.'

'Why not, if he was against getting a divorce?'

'Because he couldn't do anything to stop me.'

'Did he still love you?'

'I'm not sure he ever loved me.'

'Why would he have married you, then?'

'Maybe to be seen with a pretty, well-dressed woman. It was in Deauville, the year I was crowned Miss Europe. We ran into each other a few times in the foyer and corridors of the casino. One evening when I was at a roulette table, he pushed some big rectangular chips towards me and whispered:

' "Put that on the fourteen." '

'Did fourteen come up?'

'Not the first time, but it did the third. It came up twice in a row, and I had never seen as much money as I did that evening when I went to cash in my chips.'

The situation was reversed. It was her version of the truth that seemed the most plausible now, self-evident almost.

'He got my room number and sent me flowers. We had

dinner several times. He seemed very shy. You could tell he wasn't used to talking to women.'

'But he was thirty-five.'

'I am not that sure he'd been with any other women before me. Then he took me to Biarritz.'

'Still without asking you for anything?'

'Biarritz was like Deauville: he spent his nights in the casino then came into my room around five in the morning. Normally he didn't drink. That evening I smelled alcohol on his breath.'

'Was he drunk?'

'He had had a glass or two to work up the courage.'

'Was that when it happened?'

'Yes. He didn't stay for more than half an hour. And in the next five months, he can't have come and seen me more than a dozen times. He still asked me to marry him, though. I said yes.'

'Because he was rich?'

'Because I liked the life he led, going from hotel to hotel, casino to casino. We got married in Cannes. We continued to have separate bedrooms. He was the one who wanted it that way. He was very bashful. I think he was a bit ashamed to be so fat because he was fatter in those days than he has been recently.'

'Was he kind to you?'

'He treated me like a little girl. He didn't change his life in any way, and Ouéni, who he spent more time with than me, came everywhere with us.'

'How did you get on with Ouéni?'

'I don't like him.'

'Why?'

'I don't know. Maybe because he had too much influence on my husband. Maybe also because he's of a different religion, one which I don't understand.'

'What was Ouéni's attitude towards you?'

'He seemed not to see me. He must feel complete contempt for me, as he does for all women. One day when I was bored I asked if I could send for a Dutch maid. I put an advert in the Amsterdam papers and I chose Nelly because she seemed cheerful.'

She was smiling now, unlike her friend, who looked worried by the turn the conversation was taking.

'Let's go back to Friday evening. What time did you get back to the house?'

'Around eleven thirty.'

'Did you and Alvaredo stay at the restaurant until then?'

'No. We went to his apartment to get his suitcase. I helped him pack. We chatted and had a drink.'

'Once you got to your house, did he stay in the car?'

'Yes.'

'Did you go into the studio?'

'No. I went up to my room and got changed. I asked Nelly if Félix was downstairs, and she said she'd heard him come in.'

'Did she also tell you if he was alone or with his secretary?'

'With his secretary.'

'Didn't you have reservations about the conversation you intended to have with him because of that?'

'I was used to Ouéni always being there. I don't know

what time it was when I went downstairs. I had already put on my coat. Nelly came after me with the suitcase; she left it in the corridor. and we gave each other a hug.'

'Was she going to join you?'

'As soon as I sent word.'

'Did she go back up to her room? Without seeing how your talk turned out?'

'She knew I'd made up my mind and that I wouldn't back down.'

The telephone rang on the little round table. Maigret motioned to Lucas to pick it up.

'Hello? Yes, he's here . . . I'll put him on.'

Maigret knew he was going to hear Janvier's voice.

'He's here, chief. He's in his apartment. Boulevard . . .'

'Boulevard Montparnasse.'

'You know the address already, do you? He's got a studio apartment on the second floor. I'm in a little bar just opposite.'

'Stay there. I'll see you in a minute.'

As artless as ever, Lina asked as if it were a matter of course:

'Has Vicente got here?'

'Yes. He's in his apartment.'

'Why are the police watching him?'

'It's their job to keep all suspects under surveillance.'

'Why would he be a suspect? He never set foot in the house on Avenue du Parc-Montsouris.'

'So you say.'

'Don't you believe me?'

'I don't know when you're lying and when you're telling the truth. Incidentally, how did you get Doctor Pardon's address?'

'Nelly gave it to me. She got it from our cleaner, who lived around there. I needed to be looked at immediately and get as far from the house as possible . . .'

'Right,' he muttered, unconvinced. He wasn't taking anything for granted. 'So, you hug Nelly Velthuis in the corridor by the suitcase. She goes upstairs. You go into the studio. There you find your husband, who is working with Ouéni.'

She nodded.

'Did you talk to him about leaving straight away?'

'Yes. I told him that I was going to Amsterdam and that I would have my lawyer contact him from there to arrange the divorce.'

'How did he react?'

'He looked at me for a long time without saying anything, then muttered:

' "That can't be." '

'Didn't it occur to him to send Ouéni out of the room?'

'No.'

'Was Nahour sitting at his desk?'

'Yes.'

'With Ouéni sitting opposite him?'

'No. Ouéni was standing next to him, holding some papers. I don't remember exactly what I said. I was pretty nervous in spite of everything.'

'Did Alvaredo advise you to get a gun? Did he give you one?'

'I didn't have a gun. Why would I? I said that my decision was final and that nothing would make me change my mind and half-turned to head for the door. That's when I heard a bang and simultaneously felt a pain, like burning, in my shoulder.

'I must have looked round because I remember Félix standing, holding a pistol in his hand. I can still picture his staring eyes, as if he'd suddenly realized what he'd done.'

'What about Ouéni?'

'He was next to him, not moving.'

'What did you do?'

'I was afraid I was going to faint. I didn't want that to happen in the house, where I would be at the mercy of the two of them. I rushed for the door, found myself outside, in front of the car, and Vicente opened the door.'

'You didn't hear a second shot?'

'No. I told Vicente to drive me to Boulevard Voltaire, to a doctor I knew . . .'

'But you didn't know Doctor Pardon.'

'I didn't have time to explain. I felt very ill.'

'Why didn't you go to Alvaredo's apartment just around the corner and get him to call his doctor?'

'I didn't want a scandal. I couldn't wait to get to Holland and I was convinced the police wouldn't find out. That's why I didn't say anything at the doctor's, so no one would notice my accent.

'I wasn't expecting him to ask us any questions. I didn't even know the bullet was still in the wound. I thought it was a flesh wound, that the bleeding just had to be stopped.'

'How were you and Vicente intending to get to Amsterdam?'

'He was going to drive. When I came out of the doctor's I felt too weak to sit in a car for hours, and Vicente thought of the plane. I remembered I'd taken a night flight once. We had to wait a long time at Orly; they weren't sure whether the plane could take off because of the snow and ice.

'When we got to Amsterdam, Vicente took me straight to Anna's apartment in a taxi, and I told him of a hotel where he could wait until I had recovered. We were going to have separate rooms until the divorce.'

'To avoid being accused of adultery?'

'We didn't even need to be careful any more. After the shooting Félix couldn't refuse to divorce me.'

'So, if I've got this right, all in all this was good news for you.'

She looked at him without being able to prevent a mischievous smile crossing her face and admitted:

'Yes.'

The strangest thing was that this all held up, and he wanted to believe her, such was the apparent candour and frankness with which she answered his questions. Looking at her childlike face, like Nelly Velthuis', Maigret understood why Nahour had treated her like a little girl and why Vicente Alvaredo had fallen so in love with her that he wanted them to get married regardless of her husband and two children.

It was warm in the plush, quiet sitting room; you could easily slip into a sort of torpor. Lucas looked like a large purring cat.

'I would like to point something out, Madame Nahour: there isn't anyone to confirm your statement. According to you, there were three of you in the studio when the first shot was fired.'

'So Fouad's a witness.'

'Unfortunately for you he claims that he didn't come back to the house until after one in the morning. We have established that he left a gambling club on Boulevard Saint-Michel around that time.'

'He's lying.'

'People saw him in the club.'

'What if he went there after the shooting?'

'We'll try to check that.'

'You can ask Nelly too.'

'She doesn't understand French, does she?'

He sensed a slight hesitation before she answered indirectly:

'She speaks English.'

Suddenly Maigret's massive body seemed to unfold, and without a sound he crossed over to the door of the adjoining room, which he opened sharply. The maid almost fell into his arms and had to struggle to keep her balance.

'Have you been listening for a long time?'

On the verge of tears, she shook her head. She had changed out of her twin-piece into a black satin dress and an embroidered scalloped white apron and she was wearing a cap on her head.

'Did you understand what we were saying?'

She nodded and then shook her head, giving her employer a beseeching look.

'She understands some French,' Lina put in, 'but every time she tried to speak it, especially in the local shops, people would make fun of her.'

'Come in, Nelly. Don't stay glued to the door. How long had you known Madame Nahour was leaving for Amsterdam on Friday evening?'

'One week . . .'

'Don't look at her, look at me.'

She complied reluctantly, but still couldn't bring herself to look Maigret in the face.

'When did you pack the suitcase?'

She was clearly trying to translate the answer in her head.

'Eight o'clock.'

'Why did you lie to me when I questioned you yesterday?'

'I don't know . . . I was afraid.'

'Of what?'

'I don't know.'

'Did someone in the house frighten you?'

She shook her head, and her cap became lop-sided.

'Did you see Madame Nahour again at about ten o'clock? Where?'

'In bedroom.'

'Who brought the suitcase down?'

'I.'

'Where did your mistress go?'

'Studio.'

'Did you then hear a gunshot?'

'Yes.'

'One or two?'

She looked round for Lina again, then answered:

'One.'

'You didn't go downstairs?'

'No.'

'Why?'

She shrugged her shoulders, as if to say she didn't know. It wasn't so much that one of the women had copied the other, Maigret thought. They had each taken certain traits from the other, so that the maid now seemed to be giving a muddled version of Lina's answers.

'Did you hear Ouéni go up to his room?'

'No.'

'Did you go to sleep straight away?'

'Yes.'

'Didn't you try to find out if anyone had been hurt or killed?'

'Look through window madame. Hear door and see madame and car . . .'

'Thank you. I can only hope for your sake that when we take your statement tomorrow you won't produce a third version of events.'

The sentence was clearly too long and too difficult for her, and Madame Nahour translated it into Dutch. The young girl blushed deeply and hurriedly left the room.

'What I just said applies to you too, madame. I didn't want you to undergo an official interrogation today. I'll call tomorrow to make an appointment. I, or one of my inspectors, will come here to take down your statement.'

'There's a third witness,' she exclaimed.

'Alvaredo, I know. I'll see him when I leave here. Seeing as I don't trust the telephone, Inspector Lucas will remain in the apartment until I relieve him.'

She didn't object.

'Can I send down for something to eat? My friend Anna is always hungry. She is a real Dutchwoman. I'm going to bed.'

'Do you mind if I go into your room for a moment?'

It was in something of a mess, with clothes hastily tossed on the bed, shoes on the carpet. The telephone was plugged into the wall, like an electrical appliance. Maigret disconnected it and took it into the sitting room, then did the same with the telephone in Nelly's room.

The maid was putting underwear away in the drawers. She gave him a resentful look, as if he had reprimanded her.

'Sorry about these precautions,' he said as he took his leave of the two young women.

Lina replied with a smile:

'It's your job, isn't it?'

The porter hailed a taxi for him. A pale sun was showing behind the clouds now, and children were sliding on the icy paths in the Jardins du Luxembourg. A few had even brought toboggans.

He found the bar where Janvier was supposed to be waiting for him. He found the inspector sitting close to the misted-up window, which he wiped from time to time.

'A glass of beer,' Maigret ordered in a tired voice.

The questioning had exhausted him, and he could still feel the mugginess of the little sitting room clinging to his skin.

'Hasn't he come out?'

'No. I suppose he had lunch on the plane. He must be waiting for a telephone call.'

'He'll be waiting a while.'

Maigret could have followed his colleague from Amsterdam's example and had the telephone tapped, but maybe because he belonged to the old school, or more likely because of his upbringing, he was loath to resort to that method with anyone other than professionals.

'Lucas is staying at the Hôtel du Louvre. Come and see this young man with me. I haven't met him yet. By the way, what's he like?'

The beer was refreshing and helped him find his footing again. It was good to see a proper zinc bar with sawdust on the floor and a waiter in a blue apron.

'Very handsome, casually elegant, slightly stand-offish.'

'Did he check to see if he was being followed?'

'Not as far as I could tell.'

'Come on.'

They crossed the boulevard, went into an opulent-looking building and took the lift.

'Third floor,' said Janvier. 'I asked. He's had the studio for three years.'

There was neither a nameplate nor *carte de visite* on the door, which opened a few moments after Maigret rang. A young man, very tanned and quite tall, said with exquisite politeness:

'Come in, gentlemen. I was expecting you. Detective Chief Inspector Maigret, I imagine?'

He did not hold out his hand but led them into a light sitting room with modern furniture and paintings and a balcony roof window looking on to the boulevard.

'Won't you take your coats off?'

'One question, Monsieur Alvaredo. Madame Nahour telephoned you yesterday in Amsterdam to tell you her husband was dead. She rang again in the afternoon to tell you which plane she would be taking with her friend. You left Amsterdam this morning, and there couldn't have been anything about the case in the evening editions of the Dutch papers.'

Alvaredo turned nonchalantly to the sofa and picked up a Parisian paper from the previous day.

'They've even got your picture on the third page,' he said with a wry smile.

The two men took off their coats.

'What can I get you?'

A variety of spirits and aperitifs and several glasses stood on a low table. Only one of the glasses was to the side of the tray and still contained a little amber liquid.

'Listen carefully, Monsieur Alvaredo. Before asking you any further questions, I want to say that so far in this case I have constantly been confronted with people who take great liberties with the truth.'

'Are you talking about Lina?'

'Her and others I don't need to name. Will you first tell me the last time you were in the Nahours' house?'

'If you don't mind me saying, detective chief inspector,

that is a crude trap: excuse the expression, but it's the only one I can think of. You must know that I have never set foot in that house, either on Friday night or at any other time.'

'As far as you know, was Nahour aware of your relationship with his wife?'

'I don't know, as I only saw him two or three times, from a distance, and always at a casino table.'

'Do you know Fouad?'

'Lina has mentioned him, but I've never met him.'

'And yet on Friday evening you made no attempt to hide but waited in a very eye-catching car right in front of the gate.'

'We didn't have to hide any longer because we'd made our decision, and Lina was going to tell her husband.'

'Were you worried how their talk would turn out?'

'Why would I be? Lina had made up her mind, so he couldn't force her to stay.'

With a touch of resentment, he added:

'This isn't the Middle East.'

'Did you hear the gunshot?'

'I heard a muffled sound which I couldn't place immediately. The next moment the door opened, and Lina came rushing out on to the pavement, struggling with her suitcase. I just had time to open the door. She seemed exhausted. It was only when we'd set off that she told me everything.'

'Did you know Doctor Pardon?'

'I had never heard of him. She gave me his address.'

'Were you still planning to drive to Amsterdam?'

'I didn't know how serious her wound was. She was bleeding heavily. I was very worried.'

'Which didn't stop you lying to the doctor.'

'I thought it safer not to tell him the truth.'

'And then sneak out of his surgery.'

'So he couldn't get our names.'

'Did you know that Nahour kept a gun in the drawer of his desk?'

'Lina had never mentioned it.'

'Was she afraid of her husband?'

'He wasn't the sort of man you could be afraid of.'

'What about Ouéni?'

'She didn't say much about him.'

'But he played an important role in the house.'

'With his employer, perhaps, but he didn't have anything to do with Lina.'

'Are you sure?'

The blood suddenly rushed to Alvaredo's cheeks and ears. Through furiously gritted teeth, he replied:

'What are you implying?'

'I'm not implying anything other than that Fouad, by virtue of his influence with Nahour, could indirectly have influenced what happened to Madame Nahour.'

The young man calmed down, embarrassed that he had allowed himself to lose his temper.

'You are very passionate, Monsieur Alvaredo.'

'I'm in love . . .' he said curtly.

'May I ask how long you've been in Paris?'

'Three and a half years.'

'Are you a student?'

'I studied law in Bogotá. I came here to do a course at the Institute of Comparative Law. I also volunteer at Maître Puget's on Boulevard Raspail, just round the corner; he's a professor of international law.'

'Are your parents rich?'

'For Bogotá, yes,' he replied apologetically.

'Are you an only child?'

'I've got a younger brother who's at Berkeley in the United States.'

'Am I right in thinking that, like most Colombians, your parents are Catholic?'

'My mother is fairly devout.'

'Are you planning to take Madame Nahour to Bogotá?'

'That's my intention.'

'Don't you expect some trouble with your family if you marry a divorcee?'

'I'm an adult.'

'May I use your telephone?'

Maigret called the Hôtel du Louvre.

'Lucas? You can leave them to their own devices. But stay in the hotel. I'll send someone to relieve you at the end of the afternoon.'

Alvaredo gave a bitter smile.

'You left one of your men in Lina's room to stop her ringing me, didn't you?'

'I'm sorry I have to take these precautions.'

'I suppose your inspector will watch me too?'

'I'm not making a secret of it.'

'Can I go and see her?'

'I don't see why not.'

'The journey wasn't too trying for her, was it?'

'Not enough to make her lose any of her composure or quick-wittedness.'

'She's a child.'

'A very clever child.'

'Still no to a drink?'

'I'd rather not.'

'Meaning you still consider me a suspect?'

'It's my job to consider everyone a suspect.'

When he was outside on the pavement Maigret sighed, then took a deep breath.

'There we are!'

'Do you think he was lying, chief?'

Maigret went on without answering:

'I should get in the car if I was you. That red car will soon be racing off to Rue de Rivoli. Have a good afternoon. Keep headquarters posted so you can be relieved.'

'What about you?'

'I'm going back to Avenue du Parc-Montsouris. Tomorrow a few of us will have to conduct these interrogations officially.'

Jamming his hands in his pockets, he set off for the taxi rank on the corner of Boulevard Saint-Michel, cursing the unwieldy knitted scarf, which was making his neck itch.

The Nahours' house looked empty from the outside. Asking the taxi-driver to wait, Maigret crossed the small garden, the snow crunching under his feet, and rang the doorbell.

A sleepy Torrence let him in, yawning.

'Any news?'

'The father's here. He's in the office with his son.'

'What's he like?'

'About seventy-five, very thick white hair, wrinkled face that's still full of energy.'

The studio door opened. Recognizing Maigret, Pierre Nahour asked:

'Do you need me, detective chief inspector?'

'I'd like to see Ouéni.'

'He's upstairs.'

'Has your father seen him?'

'Not yet. I imagine he'll have some questions for him in a moment.'

Maigret hung his coat, scarf and hat on the coat rack and headed upstairs. The corridor was dark. He made his way to Fouad's room, knocked and received an answer in Arabic.

When he pushed the door open, he found Ouéni sitting in an armchair. He wasn't reading. He wasn't doing anything. The look he gave Maigret was expressionless.

'You can come in. What have they been telling you?'

6.

It was the simplest, most basic room in the house. The painter who had rented the house furnished to the Nahours must have had a teenage son, because Ouéni's bedroom was like a student's. The secretary appeared not to have changed anything, and there were no personal possessions to be seen.

Sitting in his leather armchair, legs outstretched, looking perfectly relaxed, the man was dressed as austerely as the day before in a dark, excellently cut suit. He was close-shaven. His shirt was very white, and his nails manicured.

Appearing not to notice his insolent attitude, Maigret planted himself in front of him and looked him straight in the face, as if sizing him up. The two of them were like children playing who blinks first.

'You're not very cooperative, Monsieur Ouéni.'

The secretary's face didn't betray any anxiety. If anything, he seemed to be enjoying defying Maigret with his self-assured, sarcastic smile.

'Lina . . .'

Fouad didn't let the familiarity go.

'I'm sorry?'

'Madame Nahour, if you'd rather, doesn't entirely agree with your account of what you were doing on Friday evening. She claims that when she went into the studio, you were there with Monsieur Nahour. Specifically, she says that you were standing next to him, and that he was sitting at his desk.'

Fouad smiled as Maigret waited for a reply that was not forthcoming.

'It's her word against mine, isn't it?' Fouad said eventually.

Throughout their conversation, he spoke with the same deliberate slowness, enunciating each syllable.

'Are you denying it?'

'I answered your questions yesterday.'

'That doesn't mean you told me the truth.'

Fouad's fingers tightened on the arm of his chair, as if he were reacting to an insult. Nevertheless he controlled himself and remained silent.

Maigret walked over to the window and stood in front of it for a while, then paced up and down the room with his hands behind his back and his pipe in his mouth.

'You say you left the Bar des Tilleuls just after one in the morning, which the owner confirms. But he doesn't know what time you got there. There is no proof that you didn't arrive after midnight and only looked in to give yourself an alibi.'

'Have you questioned all the club members who were in the two gaming rooms that night?'

'You know very well that we haven't had a chance to do that yet, and that today's Sunday so the club and bar are shut.'

'You have plenty of time. So do I.'

Had he adopted this attitude just to irritate Maigret? He had the coolness, the absence of nerves of a chess player, and it wasn't going to be easy to catch him out.

Maigret stopped in front of him again and asked innocuously:

'Have you been married, Monsieur Ouéni?'

The secretary replied with what might have been a proverb in his country:

'A man who isn't satisfied with the pleasures a woman can give him in one night is putting a noose around his neck.'

'Does this apply to Monsieur Nahour, say?'

'His private life is no concern of mine.'

'Do you have mistresses?'

'I'm not homosexual, if that's the question.'

His contempt was even more explicit this time.

'Meaning, I assume, that you sometimes have affairs with women?'

'If the French legal system is that curious, I can provide names and addresses.'

'You weren't seeing a woman on Friday evening, were you?'

'No. I've answered that already.'

Maigret turned back towards the window and looked vaguely at the snow-covered Avenue du Parc-Montsouris, where, despite the cold, some Sunday walkers could be seen.

'Do you own a gun, Monsieur Ouéni?'

The man stood up slowly, as if reluctant to get out of his armchair, opened the chest of drawers and took out a long, high-precision pistol. It wasn't the sort of thing you could carry in your pocket, but a practice weapon with a barrel at least twenty centimetres long. The calibre didn't match the bullet removed from Nahour's skull.

'Satisfied?'

'No.'

'Have you asked Monsieur Alvaredo the same question?'

It was Maigret's turn not to answer. The interrogation was very slow and cautious, like a game of chess, with each of the two men carefully preparing their feints and ripostes.

Maigret's face was serious. He took long pulls on his pipe, making the tobacco crackle. The silence enveloped them; no sound reached them from the muffled world outside.

'Did you know that Madame Nahour had been trying to get a divorce for almost two years?'

'I've already told you that those matters are no concern of mine.'

'Nevertheless, given how close you and Monsieur Nahour were, it's likely he talked to you about it, isn't it?'

'So you say.'

'I'm not saying anything. I'm questioning you, and you're not answering.'

'I'm answering the questions that concern me.'

'Did you also know that Madame Nahour had been planning to go to Amsterdam for more than a week, and that this would mean a final break with her husband?'

'Same comment.'

'Do you still maintain that you weren't in the room at the time of the tragedy?'

Fouad shrugged, considering the question redundant.

'You've known Nahour for twenty years or so. You

hardly left his side in all that time. He became a professional gambler, a scientific gambler one might say, and
you helped him in his calculations.'

Ouéni, who seemed not to be listening, had sat back
down in his armchair. Maigret grabbed the back of a chair
and sat astride it less than a metre from him.

'You were poor when you came to Paris, weren't you?
How much did Nahour pay you?'

'I've never been on a salary.'

'You still needed money.'

'When I did he gave it to me.'

'Do you have a bank account?'

'No.'

'How much did he give you at a time?'

'What I asked for.'

'Large amounts? Do you have savings?'

'I've never owned anything except my clothes.'

'Were you as good a gambler as him, Monsieur Ouéni?'

'It's not for me to judge.'

'Did he ever suggest you take his place at a roulette or
baccarat table?'

'Sometimes.'

'Did you win?'

'I won and lost.'

'Did you keep the winnings?'

'No.'

'So there wasn't any sort of partnership between you?
He could have given you a percentage of his winnings,
for instance.'

Ouéni's only response was a shake of the head.

'You weren't his partner or his equal, therefore, since you were completely dependent on him. So, all in all, your relationship was that of master and servant. Weren't you afraid when he got married that your relationship would become less close?'

'No.'

'Didn't Nahour love his wife?'

'You should have asked him that.'

'It's a bit late now. How long have you known that Madame Nahour has a lover?'

'Is that something I'm supposed to know?'

If he thought he was riling Maigret, he was wasting his time. Maigret had rarely been as self-possessed.

'I'm sure you know that relations between the couple, which weren't particularly close to start with, had been getting worse for two years. You must also know how insistently Madame Nahour was requesting a divorce. Did you follow her and tell your employer about her affair with Alvaredo?'

An even more contemptuous smile.

'He saw them himself as they were coming out of a restaurant in Palais-Royal. They weren't trying to hide.'

'Was Nahour furious?'

'I never saw him furious.'

'And yet, even though he was no longer sleeping with his wife and knew she was in love with someone else, he forced her to live under his roof. Wasn't that a sort of revenge?'

'Perhaps.'

'And wasn't it after he found out about the affair that

he took her children away from her and sent them to the Riviera?'

'I'm not like you, I don't read people's minds, whether alive or dead.'

'I am convinced, Monsieur Ouéni, that Madame Nahour isn't lying when she says you were with her husband on Friday evening. I would even be inclined to believe that you were aware of her trip and knew the date.'

'You're free to think what you like.'

'Her husband hated her.'

'Didn't she hate him?'

'Let's say they both hated each other. She had decided to regain her independence no matter what.'

'No matter what, exactly.'

'Are you accusing Madame Nahour of killing her husband?'

'No.'

'Are you accusing yourself?'

'No.'

'So?'

With deliberate slowness, Ouéni declared:

'There's an interested party in all this.'

'Alvaredo?'

'Where was he?'

'In his car outside.'

It was Fouad's turn to conduct the interrogation, ask the questions.

'Do you believe that?'

'Until it's proved otherwise.'

'He's a young man who's very in love, isn't he?'

Maigret let him talk, curious to see what he was driving at.

'Probably.'

'He's very passionate, isn't he? Didn't you say that he has been Madame Nahour's lover for two years? His parents will hardly welcome a divorcee with two children. The fact he's running risk implies what's called a great love, doesn't it?'

His eyes became cruel suddenly, his mouth sarcastic.

'He knew how decisive that evening would be,' he went on, sunk in his chair, as motionless as ever. 'Wouldn't you say?'

'Yes.'

'Tell me, Monsieur Maigret, if you were him, in his state of mind on Friday evening, would you have let your mistress confront her stubborn husband on her own? Do you really think he would have waited outside for almost an hour without worrying about what was going on in the house?'

'Did you see him?'

'Don't set me such crude traps. I didn't see anything because I wasn't there. I am just demonstrating that that man's presence in the studio is much more plausible than mine.'

Maigret got up, suddenly relaxed, as if they had finally got to the point.

'There were at least two people in the room,' he said in a lighter tone. 'Nahour and his wife. That would suppose that Madame Nahour was armed with a large-calibre pistol, which would have been difficult to conceal in her handbag. Nahour would also have had to fire first, and then her kill him afterwards.'

'Not necessarily. She could have fired first while her husband was holding the gun in self-defence, and it's not out of the question that he instinctively pulled the trigger as he slumped forward, which would explain the lack of accuracy . . .'

'It doesn't matter who fired first for the moment. Let's suppose you were there. Madame Nahour takes a pistol out of her bag, and, to defend your employer, you shoot in her direction, since you're standing near the drawer containing the 6.35.'

'Which would mean that then, instead of firing at me, who's armed and so can shoot her again, she fires at her husband?'

'Let's assume for the moment you loathed the man you call Monsieur Félix . . .'

'Why?'

'You've been something like a poor relation for twenty years, without even being related by blood. You have no job title but see to everything, including serving the boiled eggs in the morning. You aren't paid. You're given small amounts – pocket money, in fact – when you need it.

'I don't know if the difference of religion plays a part or not. The fact remains that there's something humiliating about your situation, and nothing breeds hatred like humiliation.

'So then the opportunity for you to avenge yourself presents itself. Nahour shoots at his wife as she's heading out of the door for the last time. You fire in your turn, not at her but at him, knowing that she or her lover will be accused. Then you just have to create an alibi for yourself at the Saint-Michel.

'We have a way, Monsieur Fouad, of working out if this is true in an hour. I'm going to call Moers, one of the best technicians at Criminal Records. If he's not at headquarters, I'll find him at home. He'll bring what's needed to carry out a paraffin test, which we've already performed on Monsieur Nahour, and we'll know from that if you've used a firearm.'

Ouéni didn't flinch. On the contrary, his smile became more sarcastic than ever. He stopped Maigret as he headed for the telephone.

'There's no point.'

'Are you confessing?'

'You know as well as I do, Monsieur Maigret, that the test can reveal powder residues on the skin up to five days after a shot has been fired.'

'Your knowledge is as varied as it is extensive.'

'On Thursday I went, as I often do, to the shooting range in the basement of a gunsmith's called Boutelleau et Fils on Rue de Rennes.'

'With your pistol?'

'No. I have another, identical one that I keep there, as many of the regulars do. It's likely therefore that you'll find powder residues on my right hand.'

'Why do you practise shooting?'

Maigret was irritated.

'Because I belong to a tribe that is armed all year round and claims to have produced the best shots in the world. Boys start firing rifles when they're ten.'

Maigret slowly looked up.

'What if we don't find powder marks on Alvaredo's or Madame Nahour's hands?'

'Alvaredo had come in from outside, where it was 12 below zero. It's safe to assume that he was wearing gloves – pretty thick ones probably – isn't it? Haven't you checked?'

He was trying to be insulting.

'I'm sorry to have to do your job for you. Madame Nahour was setting off on a journey. I assume she was wearing a coat, and it seems likely she would have already put on her gloves.'

'Is that your defence?'

'I didn't think I needed a defence until I was charged by the examining magistrate.'

'Please be at Quai des Orfèvres tomorrow morning at ten, where you will be interrogated officially. The examining magistrate you refer to may want to question you afterwards.'

'And until then?'

'You are not to leave the house, and one of my inspectors will continue to watch you.'

'I am very patient, Monsieur Maigret.'

'So am I, Monsieur Ouéni.'

Maigret's cheeks were flushed all the same as he came out of the room, although it may have been because of the heat. In the corridor, he gave a friendly nod to Torrence, who was perched on an uncomfortably hard chair, reading a magazine, then knocked on the studio door.

'Come in, Monsieur Maigret.'

The two men stood up. The older one, who was

smoking a cigar, walked towards Maigret and held out a lean, strong hand.

'I would have preferred to meet you under other circumstances, Monsieur Maigret.'

'May I offer my condolences? I didn't want to leave the house without assuring you that the Police Judiciaire and the prosecutor's office are doing everything in their power to find your son's murderer.'

'Do you have any leads?'

'I wouldn't go as far as that, but the role of everyone involved is becoming clearer.'

'Do you think Félix fired at that woman?'

'That seems indisputable, either because he voluntarily pressed the trigger, or because he did so instinctively when he was hit himself.'

The father and son looked at one another in surprise.

'Do you think that that woman, after causing him so much suffering, ended up . . .'

'I am not in a position to accuse anyone yet. Good evening, gentlemen.'

'Shall I stay?' Torrence asked moments later in the corridor.

'Fouad isn't to leave. I'd rather have you on the first floor and know of any telephone calls he makes. I don't know who'll be relieving you yet.'

The taxi-driver muttered:

'I thought you were only staying a few minutes.'

'Hôtel du Louvre.'

'Honestly, I'm not waiting for you there. I started my shift at eleven and I haven't had time to grab a bite yet.'

It was growing dark. The driver must have left his engine running from time to time because the air inside the taxi was hot.

Slumped down in the back seat, Maigret looked vaguely out at the black, chilly figures slipping along by the walls. When it came down to it, he wasn't really sure how satisfied he was with himself.

Lucas was dozing with his hands on his stomach in one of the mammoth armchairs in the lobby. Spying Maigret coming towards him through half-closed eyelids, he jumped up and asked, rubbing his eyes:

'Everything OK, chief?'

'Yes . . . No . . . Has Alvaredo shown up?'

'Not yet. None of the women has gone out. One of them, the friend, came down to the lobby to buy newspapers and magazines.'

Maigret hesitated, then grunted:

'Are you thirsty?'

'I had a glass of beer a quarter of an hour ago.'

Maigret headed to the bar on his own, left his coat, hat and scarf at the cloakroom and perched on one of the high stools. There was no one near him apart from a stand-in barman who was listening to a football match report on the radio.

'A whisky,' he ended up ordering.

He needed one before the task he had set himself. Where had he read the maxim: always attack at the point of least resistance?

It had occurred to him in the taxi. Four people knew the truth – or part of the truth – about the Nahour case. He had questioned all four of them, some twice. They had all lied, at least on one score, if not several.

Who of the four was likely to offer the least resistance?

At one moment he had thought of Nelly Velthuis, whose ingenuousness couldn't be entirely put on, but the fact that she didn't realize the seriousness of her lies meant there was no limit to what she might tell him.

Alvaredo was a likeable soul really. He was a passionate man. His love for Lina seemed sincere, even fervent, so he wouldn't say anything that might be damaging for the young woman.

Maigret had just left Ouéni, who was smart enough to anticipate and elude every trap.

That left Lina, about whom he still hadn't made up his mind. On first impression, she was a child struggling in a grown-up world, not knowing where to turn.

Starting out as a humble typist in Amsterdam, she had been attracted by the cachet of modelling before impulsively signing up for a beauty contest.

Then the miracle had happened, and overnight the young girl had found herself in a totally alien world.

A rich man, who played for high stakes every night and was fawned over by the casino staff, had sent her flowers and invited her to dinner in the best restaurants without asking for anything in return.

He took her to Biarritz, as discreetly as ever, and when he finally dared to go into her room one night, he immediately proposed marriage.

How was she supposed to understand the psychology of a man like Nahour?

Let alone Fouad Ouéni, who accompanied the couple everywhere for no obvious reason.

When she had wanted to have a Dutch maid with her, it was like a cry for help and she had chosen – from a photograph? – the most straightforward, most cheerful candidate.

She had had her pick of dresses, jewels, furs, but at Deauville, Cannes, Evian – all the places she was taken without being consulted – she was always alone and occasionally would go off to Amsterdam for heart-to-hearts with Anna Keegel, like in the old days, when the two girls shared the apartment on Lomanstraat.

She had had a child. Was she prepared for motherhood? Had Nahour brought in a nanny in case the responsibility would be too much for her?

Was that the moment she started having lovers, affairs?

The years had passed, and her features had remained as youthful, her skin as clear and smooth as ever. But what about her mind? Had she learned anything?

Another child, a son, finally satisfied her husband, who had only fleetingly tried to be close to her.

She met Alvaredo . . . Her life suddenly assumed a different complexion.

Maigret was all set to pity her, then reminded himself:

'The little girl with the innocent eyes is still the one who brought things to a head.'

And behaved surprisingly calmly since Friday evening.

He almost ordered another whisky, then decided against it and moments later took the lift up to the fourth floor. Nelly opened the door of the sitting room.

'Is Madame Nahour sleeping?'

'No. She's drinking tea.'

'Will you tell her that I want to see her.'

He found her sitting on her bed, a white silk bed jacket draped over her shoulders, leafing through an English or American magazine. The tea and cake were on the bedside table. Anna Keegel, who must have been lying on the second bed when Maigret had arrived, was smoothing down her hair and striking an attitude.

'I'd like to speak to you in private, Madame Nahour.'

'Can't Anna stay? I've never hidden anything from her, and . . .'

'Let's say her presence would make me awkward.'

It was almost true. After the door closed, Maigret moved a chair between the beds and awkwardly sat down.

'Have you seen Vicente? He's not too worried about me, is he?'

'I reassured him about your health, as you did yourself on the telephone. I imagine you're expecting him, are you?'

'In half an hour. I said I'd see him at five thirty because I was going to sleep longer. How do you think he is?'

'He seemed very in love. My first question, in fact, is about him, Madame Nahour. I realize you're doing your utmost to keep him out of this business and prevent his name being mentioned, which would complicate his and your relations with his parents in the future.

'For my part, I will spare him publicity as far as possible.

'But there is one thing that bothers me. You told me that on Friday evening he remained in the car all the time you were in the house, an hour or so.

'He knew what you'd decided. He was aware your husband refused to hear of a divorce. He had every reason therefore to think it would be a stormy, dramatic encounter. Given all that, how could he have failed to take responsibility and left you on your own?'

She was chewing her lower lip as he talked.

'It's the truth,' she merely replied.

'Ouéni thinks differently.'

'What did he tell you?'

'That Alvaredo went into the studio at the same time as you, and he added that your friend was wearing thick winter gloves. Ouéni also maintains that when your husband fired, Alvaredo took a pistol out of his pocket and fired back.'

'Ouéni is lying.'

'I would be tempted to believe that you and your husband had a bitter argument at first while Alvaredo waited discreetly by the door. When Nahour realized your decision was final, he grabbed the 6.35 from the drawer and threatened you. Your friend, thinking he was going to shoot, fired first to protect you, and Nahour pulled the trigger as he fell.'

'That's not what happened.'

'Put me right.'

'I already have. First, Vicente stayed in the car because I insisted. I even threatened not to leave with him if he set foot in the house.'

'Was your husband sitting at his desk?'

'Yes.'

'What about Ouéni?'

'He was standing to his right.'

'In front of the drawer with the revolver, then.'

'I think so.'

'You think or you're sure?'

'I'm sure.'

'Didn't Ouéni make to leave the room?'

'He started to but he didn't leave.'

'Where did he move to?'

'Into the middle of the room.'

'Before or after you started talking?'

'After.'

'You've admitted that you don't like him. Why didn't you ask your husband to send him out?'

'Félix would have refused. Besides, by then I didn't care any more.'

'How did you start?'

'I said:

' "That's it! I have made up my mind and it is final. I am leaving . . ." '

'Did you speak in French?'

'English. I learned it when I was very young; I only started speaking French much later.'

'What did your husband say?'

' "With your lover? Is that him waiting in the car?" '

'What state was Nahour in at that point?'

'He was very pale, with a hard look on his face. He slowly stood up, and I think that's when he half-opened the drawer, but I didn't know what he was intending to do yet. I said that I didn't bear him any ill will, that I was grateful for everything he'd done for me, that I'd leave it to him to decide about the children, and that my lawyer would be in touch with him.'

'Where was Ouéni?'

'I wasn't paying attention to him. Near me, I suppose. He never makes much noise.'

'Is that when your husband fired?'

'No. That was later. He repeated what he'd often told me, that he wouldn't agree to a divorce for anything. I said that he'd have to. It was only then that I realized he was holding a gun.'

'Then what happened?'

Maigret was leaning towards her slightly, as if to prevent her escaping again.

'The two . . .'

She corrected herself:

'The shot went off.'

'No. The two shots, as you were about to say. I am certain Alvaredo was in the studio, but that it wasn't him that fired.'

'Do you think it was me?'

'I don't think it was you either. Ouéni took the gun out of his pocket before or after your husband had fired.'

'There was only one shot while I was in the house, Nelly will confirm that.'

'Nelly is almost as good at lying as you are, my dear . . .'

This time the Maigret who got to his feet was almost threatening. He had stopped playing. After putting his chair back in a corner of the sitting room, he paced around the room, unrecognizable now to Lina, who had thought him almost paternal moments before.

'You'll have to stop lying at some point,' he said, 'and the sooner the better. If you don't I'll ring the examining magistrate and get an arrest warrant.'

'Why would Ouéni shoot my husband?'

'Because he loved you.'

'Him? Fouad, love someone?'

'Don't play the innocent, Lina. How long was it after you met Nahour that Ouéni became your lover?'

'Did he tell you that?'

'It doesn't matter. Answer the question.'

'Several months after my marriage. I didn't expect it. I'd never seen him with a woman. I thought he despised them.'

'Did you set out to excite him?'

'Is that what you think of me?'

'I'm sorry. Anyway, it doesn't matter if he was the one who started it. Until then he was almost Nahour's property. And now he was escaping him to a degree, through you. By becoming your lover, he was avenging himself for all past and future humiliations.'

She was suddenly almost ugly. The features of her face lost all definition, and she cried without thinking to wipe away her tears.

'You and your husband had separate rooms in the scores of hotels and villas you lived in, so it was easy for Ouéni to meet you at night. At Avenue du Parc-Montsouris . . .'

'Nothing ever happened there.'

She was genuinely distraught, looking at him with sad, beseeching eyes.

'I swear! When it became serious with Alvaredo . . .'

'What does that mean?'

'When I realized he really loved me and I loved him, I broke off everything with Fouad.'

'Who accepted it?'

'He tried everything he could, even force one time, to make me take up with him again.'

'How long ago was this?'

'Roughly a year and a half.'

'Did you know he still loved you?'

'Yes.'

'Weren't you rubbing salt into his wounds that evening by talking to your husband in front of him?'

'I didn't think of that.'

'If he moved closer to you at the start of the conversation, wasn't he trying to protect you?'

'I didn't ask myself that. I don't even really know where he was.'

'Were the two shots almost simultaneous?'

She didn't answer. She was obviously exhausted and had given up trying to maintain a pretence. Her shoulders had sunk into the pillows, and her body was curled up under the blanket.

'Why didn't you tell the truth the first time you were questioned?'

'What truth?'

'About the shot fired by Fouad.'

She answered in a whisper:

'Because I didn't want Vicente to know.'

'Know what?'

'About Fouad and me. I was ashamed. I had an affair a

long time ago in Cannes and I came clean to him about it. But not Fouad! If I accuse him, he'll tell the whole story in court, and we'll never be able to get married.'

'Wasn't Alvaredo surprised when he saw Ouéni trying to kill your husband?'

They looked straight at each other for a long time. Gradually Maigret's expression softened, while Lina's blue eyes betrayed a look of increasingly weary resignation.

'He helped me outside, and in the car I told him Fouad had always hated my husband.'

Her lower lip was slightly swollen as she added in a whisper:

'Why have you been so mean to me, Monsieur Maigret?'

7.

At eleven on Monday morning Maigret came out of one of the offices in Quai des Orfèvres after officially questioning his fourth witness.

Alvaredo had been the first. He had asked him only twenty or so questions, which Lapointe had taken down in shorthand along with the answers. One question was crucial, and the young Colombian had taken his time answering it.

'Think carefully, Monsieur Alvaredo. This will probably be the last time I'll question you before the examining magistrate takes over. Were you in your car or the house?'

'The house. Lina let me in before she went into the studio.'

'Was Nahour still alive?'

'Yes.'

'Was there anyone else in the room?'

'Fouad Ouéni.'

'Where were you standing?'

'By the door.'

'Didn't Nahour ask you to leave?'

'He pretended to ignore me.'

'Where was Fouad when the shots were fired?'

'About a metre away from Lina, in the middle of the room.'

'So, some distance from Nahour?'

'Just over three metres.'

'Who fired first?'

'I think it was Ouéni, but I'm not sure because the two shots were almost simultaneous.'

Then, as the Colombian waited for permission to leave, it had been Anna Keegel's turn in the next-door office. Their exchange had been relatively short.

In the third office he hadn't pushed Nelly Velthuis too hard. She had been surprised by everything.

'How many shots did you hear?'

'I don't know.'

'Could there have been two very close together?'

'I think so.'

As for Lina, he had made her repeat a considerable amount of what she had said the previous day, but he was careful not to allude to her affair with Fouad.

It had stopped snowing. The weather was growing milder, and the snow was turning to slush. The echoing corridor of the Police Judiciaire was as draughty as ever, but the offices were now stiflingly hot.

The whole building was filled with a sense of excitement because everyone, not just the Crime Squad, knew a major operation was underway.

Groups of journalists, including the inexorable Maquille, were sitting on the benches and pouncing on Maigret every time he came through a door.

'Later, boys. I haven't finished . . .'

A morning paper, God knows how, probably by questioning the staff at Orly, had found out about Lina's short trip to Amsterdam with a mysterious individual they called Monsieur X. This meant the case was going to take on a sensational tone, which Maigret did not like.

He still had to confront Ouéni.

On Sunday evening, when Maigret had gone home around seven after stopping by headquarters, Madame Maigret had only needed to look at him to gauge his state of mind.

'Tired?'

'It's not tiredness particularly.'

'Discouraged?'

'Damned job!' he had grunted, as he did every two or three years in situations like this. 'I'm not allowed to turn a blind eye and if I don't, I stand to ruin the lives of people who don't deserve it.'

She had taken care not to ask him any questions, and after dinner they had sat silently in front of the television.

At the far end of the corridor he took a deep breath and sighed:

'Shall we, Lapointe?'

He still had hope. He pushed open the door of the office in which Ouéni was being kept and found him, as usual, sunk in the only armchair in the room, his legs stretched out in front of him.

Like the day before, the secretary didn't stand up, didn't even greet the two men whom he looked at in turn in his cruel, sarcastic way.

Maigret remembered school lessons about Voltaire's 'hideous smile'; he had never thought it was the right word when he had looked at a bust of the great man. He had seen plenty of arrogant, aggressive, deceitful smiles since then, but this was the first time the word 'hideous' came to mind.

He went and sat on a chair, in front of a white wooden table covered with brown paper on which there was a typewriter. Lapointe sat at the side of the table and set his pad down in front of him.

'Your surname and first name.'

'Ouéni, Fouad, born in Takla, Lebanon.'

'Age?'

'Fifty-one.'

He took a residence permit from his pocket and held it out, without moving from his armchair, so Lapointe had to get up.

'I have it on the French police's authority,' he said sardonically.

'Profession?'

'Legal adviser.'

The phrase was given an even more mocking inflection.

'Your police's word again . . . Look.'

'Were you in your employer Monsieur Félix Nahour's study in Avenue du Parc-Montsouris at any point between the hours of eleven p.m. and one a.m. on Friday 14 January?'

'No. Please will you make a note that Monsieur Nahour was not my employer, as I did not receive a salary.'

'In what capacity did you accompany him to his various residences, particularly Avenue du Parc-Montsouris?'

'Friend.'

'Weren't you his secretary?'

'I helped him when he needed my advice.'

'Where were you on Friday evening after eleven?'

'At the Saint-Michel Club, where I'm a member.'

'Can you give me the names of anyone who saw you there?'

'I don't know who noticed me.'

'How many members would you say were in the club's two relatively small rooms that evening?'

'Between thirty and forty, on and off.'

'Didn't you speak to any of them?'

'No. I was there to write down winning numbers, not chat.'

'Where were you?'

'Behind the people playing. I was sitting in a corner, near the door.'

'What time did you get to Boulevard Saint-Michel?'

'Around ten thirty.'

'What time did you leave the club?'

'Around one in the morning.'

'So you are claiming that you were surrounded by over thirty people for two and a half hours, and no one noticed you?'

'I didn't say anything of the sort.'

'But you can't give any names.'

'I didn't have any dealings with the other players, who are mainly students.'

'On your way out, did you go through the bar on the ground floor? Did you talk to anyone?'

'To the landlord.'

'What did you say to him?'

'That the four came up eight times in less than an hour.'

'How did you get back to Avenue Parc-Montsouris?'

'In the car I'd come in.'

'Monsieur Nahour's Bentley?'

'Yes. I was in the habit of driving it and I could use it whenever I wanted.'

'Three witnesses say that you were in Monsieur Nahour's studio around midnight, standing to his right.'

'They all have an incentive to lie.'

'What did you do when you got back?'

'I went up to my room and went to bed.'

'Without looking into the studio?'

'That's right.'

'For the past twenty years, Ouéni, you've been living off Félix Nahour, and he's been treating you like a poor relation. You weren't just his secretary, you were also his valet and chauffeur. Didn't you find that humiliating?'

'I was grateful for his trust and did various small favours for him entirely voluntarily.'

He continued looking at Maigret defiantly, almost jubilantly. What he said could be recorded and used against him so he chose his words carefully. But it was impossible to reproduce on paper his expressions, the unrelenting look of defiance in his eyes.

'When Monsieur Nahour got married, after almost fifteen years living alone with you, didn't you feel frustrated?'

'Our relationship wasn't inspired by passion, if that's what you're insinuating. I had no reason to be jealous.'

'Did your employer have a happy marriage?'

'He didn't confide in me about his married life.'

'Do you think, particularly during the last two years,

that Madame Nahour was satisfied with the life she was leading with her husband?'

'I've never given it a thought.'

Maigret's gaze became more insistent this time, as if conveying a message, and Ouéni understood it. As a kind of silent challenge, he maintained his cynical attitude, which contrasted sharply with the neutral tone of his answers.

'What was your relationship with Madame Nahour?'

'I didn't have anything to do with her.'

Now that the interrogation was official, with a crucial bearing on how the case would turn out, every word was loaded with dynamite.

'Didn't you try to seduce her?'

'The thought never occurred to me.'

'Have you ever been alone in a room with her?'

'If you mean a bedroom, the answer is no.'

'Think.'

'It's still no.'

'A 7.65 calibre gun was found in your room. Do you have another pistol, and, if so, where is it now?'

'At a gunsmith's in Rue de Rennes, where I often go and practise.'

'When did you go there last?'

'Thursday.'

'Thursday the 13th, the day before the murder, that is. Did you know at the time that Madame Nahour was intending to leave her husband the next day?'

'She didn't confide in me.'

'Her maid knew.'

'We weren't on very good terms, Nelly and I.'

'Because you propositioned her, and she rejected you?'

'More the other way around.'

'So, in a word, this shooting session on Thursday comes in very handy for explaining why you most probably have powder residues on your fingers. At least two people were in Monsieur Nahour's studio on Friday evening, just before or just after midnight. Both swear under oath that you were also there.'

'Who are these two people?'

'Madame Nahour, for one.'

'What was she doing there?'

'She had come to tell her husband that she was leaving that night and to ask for a divorce.'

'Did she tell you that her husband was prepared to grant her this divorce? Was it the first time she'd talked to him about it? Didn't she know he would do everything he could to oppose it?'

'Including shooting her?'

'Has it been proved that he shot intentionally? After all, in your experience is it usual to aim at someone's throat from a distance of three or four metres? Did Madame Nahour also tell you why she was suddenly so impatient to get a divorce?'

'To marry Vicente Alvaredo, who was with her in the room when the shots were fired.'

'Shot or shots?'

'There were two almost simultaneous shots, and it seems to have been the first that hit Nahour in the throat.'

'Which implies the second shot was fired by a dead man, doesn't it?'

'His death wasn't necessarily instantaneous. Nahour could have instinctively pulled the trigger as he was suffering massive blood loss and staggering, about to fall.'

'Who is supposed to have fired the first shot?'

'You.'

'Why?'

'Perhaps to protect Lina Nahour, perhaps out of hatred for your employer.'

'Why not Alvaredo?'

'He's apparently never used a gun in his life and doesn't have one. The investigation will confirm this one way or the other.'

'They fled the scene, didn't they?'

'They went to Amsterdam, as they had been planning to for a week, and returned to Paris as soon as the Dutch police advised them to do so.'

'Was that your doing? Had you promised they wouldn't be bothered? Monsieur Alvaredo was wearing gloves, wasn't he?'

'That's correct.'

'Weren't they thick leather gloves that haven't been found?'

'They were found yesterday evening at Orly, and the laboratory hasn't found any traces of gunpowder on them.'

'Wasn't Madame Nahour, who was going away, wearing gloves too?'

'Again the test produced nothing.'

'Are you sure they're the same gloves?'

'The maid says they are.'

'You mentioned three witnesses at the start. I suppose the third is Nelly Velthuis?'

'She heard the two shots from the corridor on the first floor, where she was leaning over the banisters, waiting for them to finish their conversation.'

'Did she tell you that on Saturday?'

'That's none of your concern.'

'Can you at least tell me where she spent the day on Sunday?'

'At the Hôtel du Louvre, with her employer and a friend of hers.'

'Did these three people have any visitors apart from you? I imagine you went to question them, as you did me in Avenue du Parc-Montsouris.'

'Alvaredo went to see them in the late afternoon.'

Switching roles, Ouéni then said curtly:

'That's enough. From now on I'll only talk in the presence of my lawyer.'

'There's a question I've already asked you, though, and I insist on doing so again: what was the exact nature of your relationship with Madame Nahour?'

Ouéni gave an icy smile. His eyes were darker and brighter than ever as he spat:

'Non-existent.'

'Thank you. Lapointe, will you call two inspectors?'

He had got up, walked round the desk and was standing in front of Ouéni, who was still sunk in his armchair. Looking him up and down, Maigret asked bitterly:

'Revenge?'

After checking they were alone in the room and that the door was shut, Fouad said:

'Possibly.'

'Stand up.'

He obeyed.

'Hold out your wrists.'

He did so, still smiling.

'I arrest you on a warrant from Examining Magistrate Cayotte.'

Turning to the two inspectors who had come in, Maigret went on:

'Take this man to the cells.'

8.

It had become 'the Nahour case'. For a week it was deemed worthy of the front pages of all the newspapers and several columns in the scandal sheets. Journalists haunted Avenue Parc-Montsouris, gathering tittle-tattle, and Madame Bodin, the cleaner, had her hour of glory.

Maquille went to Amsterdam, then Cannes, returning with an interview with the nanny and a photograph of her and the children. He questioned the casino managers and croupiers while he was at it.

In the meantime men from Criminal Records went over the Nahours' house with a fine-tooth comb in the hope of finding a clue. The garden likewise; even the drains were searched in the hope of finding the pistol that had been used to kill Nahour.

The meeting at the lawyer's took place on Monday afternoon, with Pierre Nahour, his father and Lina attending.

Maître Leroy-Beaudieu telephoned Maigret to fill him in. In his second will, Félix Nahour left his wife the bare legal minimum. Everything else went to his children, and he expressed the wish that they would be entrusted to his brother's care, or, if that was impossible, that he would be made a surrogate guardian.

'Didn't he leave anything to Ouéni?'

'I was struck by that. I can tell you now that, in his first will, which was voided by the second, Nahour left a sum of five hundred thousand francs to his secretary "for his devotion and services". The name Ouéni isn't even mentioned in the final will.'

Had Nahour found out about Fouad's affair with Lina in the meantime?

Thirty-six of the Saint-Michel's regulars, along with its manager and its croupiers all testified before the examining magistrate.

Journalists were waiting for them as they came out, which led to incidents after some of the witnesses rushed furiously at the photographers.

There were some mistakes too. A Cambodian student claimed to have seen Ouéni sitting in the corner from 11 p.m. onwards. It took two days of patient checking to establish that the student had got confused with the previous Wednesday and hadn't been in the club on Friday.

Various neighbours, who had come back from the cinema at around 11.30, swore they hadn't seen any cars parked outside the bar.

Examining Magistrate Cayotte was a meticulous, patient man. For three months he called Maigret into his office almost every day with new questions for him to investigate.

Politics reasserted its hold over the newspapers, and the Nahour case was relegated to the third, then the fifth page, before disappearing completely.

Lina, Alvaredo and Nelly were forbidden to leave Paris without permission, and it was only after the investigation was finished that they were allowed to retreat to a little house near Dreux.

The Court of Indictment confirmed Ouéni's indictment, but the Assizes Court was so busy the trial only took place in January the following year, a year after Doctor Pardon had seen the mute shooting victim and her lover in his surgery on Boulevard Voltaire.

Strangely, in the interim the two men had avoided referring to the Nahours at their monthly dinners.

Finally the day came when a slightly flushed Maigret had to give evidence in court. Until then nothing had been said about Lina's affair with the defendant.

Maigret answered the presiding judge's questions as briefly and factually as possible. When he saw the prosecutor get to his feet, he knew the young woman's secret was in danger.

'Will Your Honour allow me to put a question to the witness?'

'The state prosecutor has the floor.'

'Can the witness tell the jury if it has come to his knowledge that, at an as yet unspecified time, the defendant and Madame Nahour were intimate with one another?'

Maigret was testifying under oath; he couldn't conceal anything.

'Yes.'

'Has the defendant denied this formally?'

'Yes.'

'Nevertheless his attitude suggests it was the truth?'

'Yes.'

'Did the witness believe in this relationship?'

'Yes.'

'Didn't this conviction play a part in Ouéni's arrest by shedding new light on his motives?'

'Yes.'

That was all. The spectators had listened in silence, but now there was an uproar in court, and the presiding judge had to use his gavel.

'If order is not restored immediately, I shall clear the court.'

Maigret could have gone and sat next to Cayotte, who had kept him a seat, but he preferred to leave the court.

When he was alone in the deserted corridor, his footsteps echoing in the silence, he slowly filled a pipe without realizing what he was doing.

A few moments later he was sitting in the refreshment room of the Palais, where he gruffly ordered a glass of beer.

He couldn't face going home. He drank another glass, almost in one, then slowly made for Quai des Orfèvres.

There was no snow this year. The air was mild. It felt like early spring, and the sun was so bright you expected to see the buds bursting into flower.

When he got to his office, he opened the door to the inspectors' room.

'Lucas! Janvier! Lapointe!'

It was as if all three had been waiting for him.

'Put on your coats and come with me.'

They set off without asking where he was taking them. A few minutes later they were climbing the worn steps of the Brasserie Dauphine.

'Well, Monsieur Maigret, what about this Nahour case, then?' the landlord asked him.

He regretted it immediately. Maigret just looked at him with a shrug, and he quickly added:

'We've got andouillette today, you know.'

There was going to be no trip to Bogotá for the couple now. And after the morning's hearing would Lina and Alvaredo's relationship ever be the same again?

The Nahour case was back on the front pages. The evening papers were already talking about a *ménage à quatre*.

If it hadn't been for the new motive, which was the centrepiece of the prosecution's summing-up, the jury might have voted to acquit.

The gun hadn't been found. Everything rested on the testimony of more or less interested parties.

The following evening, Fouad Ouéni was sentenced to ten years in prison, while Lina and Alvaredo, who had been taken out through a side door, got into the Alfa Romeo and drove off to an unknown destination.

Maigret heard nothing more about them.

'I failed,' he had to admit to Pardon the following Tuesday at dinner at the doctor's apartment.

'Maybe if I hadn't called you that night . . .'

'Events would have still run their course, it just would have taken a little longer.'

Reaching for his glass of Marc de Bourgogne, Maigret added:

'Ouéni won, really.'

OTHER TITLES IN THE SERIES

MAIGRET AND THE TRAMP
GEORGES SIMENON

'Maigret was devoting as much of his time to this case as he would to a drama keeping the whole of France agog. He seemed to be making it a personal matter, and from the way he had just announced his encounter with Keller, it was almost as if he was talking about someone he and his wife had been anxious to meet for a long time.'

When a Paris tramp known as 'Doc' is pulled from the Seine after being badly beaten, Maigret must delve into the past to discover who wanted to kill this mysterious figure.

Translated by Howard Curtis

Other Titles in the Series

MAIGRET'S ANGER
GEORGES SIMENON

'*There was a dressing table painted grey and cluttered with jars of cream, make-up, eyeliner. The room had a stale, faintly sickly smell. This was where the performers swapped their everyday clothes for their professional gear before stepping out into the spotlights, out to where men bought champagne at five or six times the going rate for the privilege of admiring them.*'

Maigret is perplexed by the murder of a Montmartre nightclub owner, until he uncovers a crime much closer to home that threatens his own reputation.

Translated by Will Hobson

OTHER TITLES IN THE SERIES

MAIGRET AND THE GHOST
GEORGES SIMENON

'It wasn't a traditional painter's smock that Madame Jonker was wearing. It was more a monk's habit, the fabric as thick and soft as a bathrobe.

The Dutchman's wife also wore a white turban of the same fabric around her head.

She was holding a palette in her left hand, a brush in her right, and her black eyes lighted on Maigret with curiosity.'

The shooting of a fellow inspector and the disappearance of a key witness lead Maigret to some disturbing discoveries about an esteemed Paris art critic.

Translated by Ros Schwartz

OTHER TITLES IN THE SERIES

MAIGRET DEFENDS HIMSELF
GEORGES SIMENON

'*Maigret's cheeks turned red, as they had at school whenever he was called to the headmaster's office. 28 June ... He had been in the Police Judiciaire for more than thirty years, and the head of the Crime Squad for ten years, but this was the first time he had been summoned like this.*'

When Maigret is shocked to find himself accused of a crime, he must fight to prove his innocence and save his reputation.

Translated by Howard Curtis

OTHER TITLES IN THE SERIES

MAIGRET'S PATIENCE
GEORGES SIMENON

'Maigret felt less light at heart than when he had woken up that morning with sunlight streaming into his apartment or when he had stood on the bus platform, soaking up images of Paris coloured like in a children's album. People were often very keen to ask him about his methods. Some even thought they could analyse them, and he would look at them with mocking curiosity.'

When a gangster Maigret has been investigating for years is found dead in his apartment, the Inspector continues to bide his time and explore every angle until he finally reaches the truth.

Translated by David Watson

www.penguin.com

OTHER TITLES IN THE SERIES